Classic of Poetry

Shi Jing

ISBN: 9798863825519

Imprint: Daybreak Studios

CONTENTS

PREFACE

"The Book of Songs," also known as the "Classic of Poetry" or "Shi Jing," is a timeless collection of Chinese poetry that spans over two millennia. This anthology, which dates back to the early Zhou Dynasty (c. 11th to 7th century BCE), is not only one of China's most significant literary treasures but also a window into the soul of Chinese culture and history.

In these verses, we encounter the echoes of ancient Chinese sentiments, dreams, and observations. From themes of love and longing to the joys and sorrows of daily life, the "Book of Songs" offers us a glimpse into the rich tapestry of human emotions and experiences.

As we delve into the pages of this revered work, we are transported to a world where the beauty of language and the depth of human expression converge. It is a testament to the enduring power of poetry to capture the essence of a people and a nation.

In this English translation of the "Book of Songs," we strive to preserve the beauty and significance of these verses, offering readers a bridge to the heart of Chinese culture and an appreciation for the timeless artistry of its poets. May this work serve as a source of inspiration and insight into the enduring spirit of China's literary heritage.

GUO FENG (国风)

Zhu Xi's "Poetry Commentary" says: "Guo (国) refers to the territories granted to feudal lords, and Feng (风) refers to the songs and poems of the people's customs." This means that Guo Feng refers to the poems of various feudal states. So, why are these poems called "Feng"? "The Preface to the Book of Songs" explains: "Feng means wind, which also means teaching. Wind moves things, and teaching transforms them. ... The rulers use wind to influence the people below, and the people use wind to advise those above. When one speaks with skillful persuasion, the speaker is without guilt, and the listener can be sufficiently warned. Therefore, it is called 'Feng.'" Zhu Xi further explains: "Just as things produce sound due to the movement of the wind, and that sound can also affect living creatures." This refers to the function of poetry. There are fifteen Guo Feng in total, which are Zhou Nan, Shao Nan, Bei, Yong, Wei, Wang, Zheng, Qi, Wei, Tang, Qin, Chen, Hui, Cao, and Bin.

ZHOU NAN (周南)

Zhou refers to a place name (or some say a state name), located south of Mount Qi in Yongzhou. It was the fief of Duke Ji Dan of Zhou and covers parts of present-day southwestern Henan and northwestern Hubei. These poems were mostly written in the late Western Zhou and early Eastern Zhou periods. There are eleven extant poems in this category, and they predominantly deal with themes of marriage, love, and customs.

GUAN JU (关雎)

The ospreys cry out, oh, oh!
Perched and resting on the river's sandbar.
A beautiful and virtuous maiden,
Truly a fitting partner for a noble gentleman.

Long and short, the pickerelweed grows,
Harvested on the left and on the right.
The beautiful and virtuous maiden,
In dreams, I cannot forget her.

Beautiful hopes are hard to realize,
Awake, I still yearn for her.
Thinking this way and that,
Tossing and turning, I can't sleep.

Long and short, the pickerelweed grows,
Harvested on the left and on the right.
The beautiful and virtuous maiden,
Plays the zither and makes music, expressing her love.

Long and short, the pickerelweed grows,
Harvested on the left and on the right.
The beautiful and virtuous maiden,
Rings the bells and beats the drums to make her happy.

GE TAN (葛覃)

Ge plants, long vines and tendrils grow,
Stretching through the valleys below.
Leaves lush green and verdant show.
Yellow birds flutter high and low,
Perching on bushes in a joyful flow,
Their songs resound like a melodious crow.

Ge plants, long vines and tendrils grow,
Stretching through the valleys below.
Leaves dense and rich, a bountiful row.
Harvested and boiled to and fro,
Stripped into fine threads to bestow,
Wearing Ge clothes, comfort in tow.

Going back, I'll tell my mentor, you know,
I must ask for leave to my parents go.
First, wash the inner clothes in the row,
Then the outer garments, all aglow.
Washed or not, neatly arranged, you'll show,
When I return, to my parents I'll bow.

JUAN ER (卷耳)

Picking and picking, the Juan Er I've found,
Never enough to fill my basket's mound.
Because I yearn for someone far from this ground,
I scatter the baskets by the roadside, unbound.

As I ascend to the mountain's peak, all around,
My horse's legs grow weak, slowing down.
Let's fill the wine cup, in sorrow, I drown,
Drinking to forget, in a tipsy renown.

Again, I climb the hill, my horse's gown,
Fatigued and worn, in shades of brown.
Let's fill the wine cup, let sorrow be thrown,
Drinking to oblivion, woes disown.

Once more, I climb a rocky mound,
My horse is worn out, lying on the ground.
Servants are weary, journeying bound,
When will my sorrows finally unbound?

JIU MU (樛木)

In the south, there's a tree, curved and grand,
Its branches entwined with green vines, so grand.
For the joyful gentleman, a wish so grand,
May happiness grace him, bless his land.

In the south, there's a tree, verdant and grand,
Its leaves and tendrils in abundance, so grand.
For the joyful gentleman, a wish so grand,
May happiness protect him, as he expands.

In the south, there's a tree, lush and grand,
With Ge vines twining, green and grand.
For the joyful gentleman, a wish so grand,
May happiness make his achievements grand.

ZHONG SI (螽斯)

Zhong Si, with wings in flight,
In the sky, a bustling sight.
Your offspring, oh, so bright,
Your lineage thrives, with all your might.

Zhong Si, wings in motion, so light,
In the air, a buzzing might.
Your offspring, always in sight,
Generations follow, in endless light.

Zhong Si, wings flapping, unite,
In groups, soaring to new heights.
Your offspring, in harmony, unite,
Living together, joyful and bright.

TAO YAO (桃夭)

The peach tree, with lush leaves and branches wide,
Its flowers in pink, a radiant sight.
The maiden is soon to be a bride,
May her husband's home be harmonious and bright.

The peach tree, with lush leaves and branches wide,
Its peaches plump, sweet, and bona fide.
The maiden is soon to be a bride,
May her husband's home be joyful, no divide.

The peach tree, with lush leaves and branches wide,
Its leaves dance in the breeze, side by side.
The maiden is soon to be a bride,
May her husband's home be prosperous, a pleasant ride.

TU JU (兔罝)

A hunting net with intricate mesh,
Securely fastened to a wooden post, fresh.
The mighty warriors, brave and bold,
Defending lords and nobles, their story told.

A hunting net with intricate mesh,
Deployed where crossings intermesh.
The mighty warriors, brave and true,
Guarding lords and nobles, the chosen few.

A hunting net with intricate mesh,
Set among dense woods, a safety address.
The mighty warriors, loyal and grand,
Beloved by lords, they proudly stand.

FU YI (芣苢)

Plantain seeds, oh, gather and amass,
Quickly bring them, no time to surpass.
Plantain seeds, oh, pick them from the grass,
Hurry, collect them, let nothing pass.

Plantain seeds, oh, gather and retrieve,
Swiftly, don't let any of them leave.
Plantain seeds, oh, pick them without reprieve,
Swiftly, gather them up, don't deceive.

Plantain seeds, oh, gather them in a heap,
Swiftly, collect them, don't let them seep.
Plantain seeds, oh, gather them in a sweep,
Swiftly, bring them all, no time to sleep.

HAN GUANG (汉广)

In the south, there's a tree, tall and grand,
Resting beneath it, hard to withstand.
A maiden in Han, so far away,
To pursue her, the journey's a lengthy way.

The Han River, wide and vast,
Swimming across is no easy task.
The Yangtze, swift and long,
How can a wooden raft get us along?

In the fields, the weeds grow tall,
To gather firewood, we must stand tall.
If the maiden becomes my wife, my all,
I'll make sure her horse is well-fed, overall.

The Han River, wide and vast,
Swimming across is no easy task.
The Yangtze, swift and long,
How can a wooden raft get us along?

In the fields, the weeds grow tall,
To gather firewood, we must give our all.
If the maiden becomes my wife, my call,
I'll make sure her horse is content, after all.

The Han River, wide and vast,
Swimming across is no easy task.
The Yangtze, swift and long,
How can a wooden raft get us along?

RU FEN (汝坟)

Walking along the banks of the Ru River, I tread,
Cutting wood branches to burn, it is said.
Long have I yearned for my husband's return,
Like a morning's hunger, it continues to churn.

Walking along the banks of the Ru River, I go,
Felling fresh branches from trees in a row.
Finally, my husband's return I discern,
No longer far away, he'll stay in turn.

The red tail of the redfin chub does unfold,
The ruler's oppressive rule, like fire, is bold.
Though oppression burns, hot and cold,
I'm fortunate to reunite with parents, the stories told.

LIN ZHI ZHI (麟之趾)

The feet of a Qilin, they don't kick or fight,
Energetic young lords, full of might,
Oh, you all resemble the Qilin's light!

The forehead of a Qilin, it doesn't bump or smite,
Energetic kinsmen, standing upright,
Oh, you all resemble the Qilin's height!

The horns of a Qilin, they don't hurt or bite,
Energetic clansmen, virtuous and right,
Oh, you all resemble the Qilin's might!

SHAO NAN (召南)

Shao is a place name, situated to the west of Mount Qi. When King Wu established his rule, he enfeoffed Ji Shi in the Shao region, which is now in the southwestern part of present-day Qishan County, Shaanxi Province. Ji Shi was given the title of Duke of Shao or Shao Bo. During the reign of King Cheng, Duke of Shao and Duke of Zhou divided the Shao region for governance. Duke of Shao ruled the western part of Shao, while Duke of Zhou ruled the eastern part. Shao Nan refers to the southern vassal states west of Shao. The poems in "Shao Nan" mostly originated from this region. There are currently fourteen poems in this category, and they often revolve around themes of marriage, longing for loved ones, and labor, including hunting.

QUE CHAO (鹊巢)

The magpies build their nests high in the tree,
And the mynah birds come to live with glee.
This maiden is about to wed, you see,
A hundred carriages come to accompany.

The magpies build their nests high in the tree,
And the mynah birds join in harmoniously.
This maiden is about to wed, you'll agree,
A hundred carriages come to ensure security.

The magpies build their nests high in the tree,
And the mynah birds live there abundantly.
This maiden is about to wed, joyfully,
A hundred carriages come for her ceremony.

CAI FAN (采蘩)

Where shall we gather the white mugwort's grace?
By the pond, in the marshy, watery place.
Why do we gather this herb's embrace?
To feed silkworms and maintain a steady pace.

Where shall we gather the white mugwort's grace?
In the mountain stream, a fertile trace.
Why do we gather this herb's embrace?
To send to the lord's silkworm room, we chase.

Silkworm wives with their hair neatly coiled,
Day and night, their silkworms carefully toiled.
When evening comes, their hair is disarrayed,
Rushing back home, their worries displayed.

CAO CHONG (草虫)

The grasshoppers chirp in the grassy land,
Locusts hop and jump in the sand.
Long have I not seen my husband's hand,
My heart is anxious, in sorrow I stand.

If one day I see him as I planned,
If I meet him, my joy will expand,
Only then will my heart truly understand.

I climb the high southern mountain's crest,
Gather ferns in the greenest of forest.
Long have I not seen my husband, distressed,
My heart's grief cannot be suppressed.

If one day I see him, feeling blessed,
If I meet him, my heart will be at rest,
And the pain within my soul will be addressed.

CAI PIN (采蘋)

Where do we gather water shield plants green?
By the stream in the southern mountain scene.
Where do we collect water moss so serene?
In pools and marshes, lush and pristine.

How do we carry the water shield sheen?
Round baskets and square crates, a routine.
How do we cook the plants we convene?
In three-legged pots and cauldrons, it's seen.

Where do we present this offering keen?
In the ancestral temple's window-screen.
Who will officiate this ritual's theme?
With respect and devotion, the maiden we've seen.

GAN TANG (甘棠)

The Gan Tang tree, so tall and grand,
Do not prune its branches, don't disband.
The Duke of Shao once took a stand,
Slept beneath it in this land.

The Gan Tang tree, so tall and grand,
Do not trim its branches by your hand.
The Duke of Shao in peace did stand,
Resting beneath its branches so grand.

The Gan Tang tree, so tall and grand,
Do not pluck its branches or demand.
The Duke of Shao's repose was planned,
Beneath its branches, where he'd land.

XING LU (行露)

Dew on the road, wet and cold,
I can't help but wish I'd left days old.
But dew on the road, it's hard to uphold,
Who says that birds have no bills, I'm told.

Why have they pecked through my roof's fold?
Who says they never had a home, I'm bold.
Even though they've caused this household,
I'll never marry one of their brood, I scold.

Who says that mice have no teeth so old,
How did they pierce my walls, so untold?
Who says they never had a home to hold,
Now they've forced me into the courts, I'm told.
Even though they've taken me into their fold,
I'll never marry one of their kin, I hold.

LAMB (羔羊)

In a lamb-skin robe so finely sewn,
White silk threads in patterns carefully sown.
With a full belly, I leave the gate on my own,
Leisurely and carefree, I roam alone.

In a lamb-skin robe so finely sewn,
White silk threads in patterns beautifully shown.
Leisurely and carefree, my heart has grown,
With a full belly, I return to my own.

In a lamb-skin robe so finely sewn,
White silk threads in patterns skillfully known.
Leisurely and carefree, I'm on my own,
Exiting the gate, with food and drink overflown.

YIN QI LEI (殷其雷)

Rolling thunder resounds on the slope of the southern mountain,
Why did you leave home at this hour? It's not known.
My honest husband, where have you gone?
Go back home quickly, don't stay on your own!

Rolling thunder resounds near the southern mountain,
Why did you leave home, not at ease to roam?
My honest husband, please don't delay,
Hurry back home, without further delay!

Rolling thunder resounds at the foot of the southern hill,
Why did you leave home, not enjoying your fill?
My honest husband, why this long absence still?
Hurry back home, our hearts to fulfill!

BIAO YOU MEI (摽有梅)

Plum trees ripe, their fruits fall like snow,
On the branches, still, some fruits do glow.
Young men seek me, don't let the chance go,
While plums are fresh, it's time to bestow.

Plum trees ripe, their fruits in the flow,
On the branches, some fruits still show.
Young men seek me, let your intentions show,
While the day is bright, let love's river flow.

Plum trees ripe, their fruits in a row,
With a basket in hand, I bend low.
Young men seek me, let your love grow,
Speak your heart's desire and let it flow.

XIAO XING (小星)

Tiny stars flicker in the sky,
Three by three, five by five, up high.
Hastily, I travel, oh my,
Morning and night, no time to sigh.

Our destinies differ, by and by.
Tiny stars flicker in the night sky,
Clustered and bright, up high they fly.
Hastily, I travel, oh so spry,
With my blanket and bed, nearby.

Others have better fates, oh why?

JIANG YOU SI (江有汜)

The river flows wide, with a tributary near,
My husband's returning, no need to fear.
Why leave me home, shedding a tear?
Don't let our happiness disappear here.

The river's so wide, with a stream quite clear,
My husband's coming, please draw near.
Why abandon me, my love so dear?
Don't let our love turn insincere.

The river rushes on, a tributary near,
My husband's journey, I hold dear.
Why depart, leaving behind your sphere?
Don't let my heartache turn into a sneer.

YE YOU SI LUO (野有死麕)

I killed a fawn in the wilderness so remote,
Wrapped it in white grass to keep it afloat.
A young lad seeking me by anecdote,
Let's talk now, before it's too late.

I cut down a sapling to burn in a gloat,
I killed a fawn in the wilderness, no dote.
Wrapped in white grass, a gift remote,
For the fair maiden, I devote.

"Take your time, don't hastily bloat,
Don't let the apron make a fuss or denote,
Don't let the dog bark, throat to throat."

HE BI PENG YI (何彼襛矣)

Why is it so rich and beautifully bright?
Like blooming peonies, a glorious sight.
Why isn't there a dignified aura in flight?
This is the carriage for the royal bride's rite.

Why is it so rich and beautifully bright?
Like apricot and plum blossoms, sheer delight.
On the carriage, a nobleman sits upright,
A princess of Qi, to become a bride tonight.

ZOU YU (驺虞)

From the lush reeds around and about,
I've driven a herd of wild boars out.
Oh, what a wonderful animal to tout!

From the thick growth of sedges, no doubt,
I've chased a litter of wild boars, devout.
Oh, what a wonderful animal to shout!

From the dense reeds all about,
I've driven a troop of wild boars, no clout.
Oh, what a wonderful animal to flout!

BEIFENG (邶风)

Beifeng is a collection of poems from the state of Bei, which was one of the three states formed after the fall of the Shang dynasty, along with Yong and Wei. These states were located in the vicinity of Chaoge. Following King Wu's defeat of the Shang dynasty, the northern part of Chaoge became Bei, the eastern part became Yong, and the southern part became Wei. Later, the territories of Bei and Yong were absorbed into the state of Wei. Therefore, the "Beifeng," "Yongfeng," and "Weifeng" poems are collectively known as the "Weishishi" (卫诗), and most of them were composed during the Eastern Zhou period.

These poems often express resistance to and expose the immoral actions of the ruling elite. For example, "Yongfeng·Xiangshu" (鄘风·相鼠), "Yongfeng·Qiang You Ci" (鄘风·墙有茨), and "Beifeng·Xintai" (邶风·新台) criticize the rulers. They also reflect the fate of women and their spirit of resistance in the context of marriage and love. Examples include "Beifeng·Bai Zhou" (邶风·柏舟), "Weifeng·Mang" (卫风·氓), and "Beifeng·Gu Feng" (邶风·谷风). There are currently nineteen surviving poems in the "Beifeng" collection.

BAI ZHOU (柏舟)

Upon the river's gentle, swaying boat of cypress wood,
I drift along the waves, as best I could.
My heart with worries, sleep does not elude,
For hidden sorrows, my thoughts are glued.

It's not that there's no wine at home to brood,
Or places to roam, where spirits can be viewed.
My heart's not a mirror, as you've construed,
It can't reflect all, whether bad or good.

In my family, I've brothers, understood,
But relying on them, it's not as it should.
I've poured out my heart, my pain reviewed,
But they were angry, their anger brewed.

My heart's not a stone, to be misconstrued,
Not for you to toss, or with words intrude.
My heart's not a mat, to be unrolled and viewed,
I have my dignity, don't misconstrue.

Sorrows wrap around me, like tangled wood,
Petty people see me as their feud.
Malice and schemes, they have pursued,
Their insults and slights, it's not subdued.

With careful thought, my worries renewed,
I wake and pound my chest in solitude.
I ask the sun and moon, oh, the magnitude,
Why do they take turns, darkness imbued?

My heart's filled with worries, it's not subdued,
Like wearing dirty clothes, feeling subdued.
With careful thought, my worries reviewed,

I can't soar high, with wings so renewed.

GREEN ROBES (绿衣)

Oh, that green-colored attire,
Outside green, inside yellow, in its entire.
Seeing this garment, my heart feels dire,
Sorrow and grief, when will they expire?

That green attire, so distinct,
Above, green, below, yellow, as I think.
Seeing this garment, my heart does sink,
When will I forget this feeling's link?

The green threads in your hand, so tight,
Mending my heart, like day and night.
Thinking of my departed wife so bright,
Always advising me to act just right.

With coarse and fine fabric, made with grace,
Wearing it, cool and breezy is the place.
Thinking of my departed wife's embrace,
Everything aligns with my heart's pace.

SWALLOW (燕燕)

Swallows in pairs soar high and wide,
Their formation uneven, wings open wide.
She returns home, on this we bide,
Sent far away to the wilderness, outside.

Gradually, she vanishes from our sight,
Tears flow like rain, in sadness and fright.

Swallows in pairs ascend the sky,
Up and down, they sing and fly.
She returns home, we let her comply,
Not fearing the long journey, oh my!

Gradually, she fades from our sight,
Tears pool in my eyes, a woeful plight.

Swallows in pairs, in the heavens, they glide,
Up and down, they chirp like a guide.
She returns home, her path she does stride,
Sent southward, where roads open wide.

Gradually, she vanishes from our sight,
My heart aches, a pain taking flight.

ZHONGSHI (仲氏)

Zhongshi is honest, truly reliable,
Open-hearted, patient, her spirit undeniable.
Gentle in nature, never to belie,
Good in her actions, thoughtful in her reply.

She often said, "Remember our dear past,"
Her counsel, in my heart, it did last.
She is a model from which I'm cast,
In her memory, my love forever steadfast.

SUN AND MOON (日月)

The sun and moon shine their radiant light,
Illuminating the earth so bright.
But there are people who, out of spite,
Defy tradition, causing harm despite.

When will normalcy return to sight?
They disregard my feelings, as if it's right.

The sun and moon in the sky's great height,
Radiance fills the day and night.
But people like them, oh, what a blight,
Abandoning virtue, ending our plight.

When will normalcy return to light?
Can they forget my sorrow overnight?

The sun and moon shine with all their might,
Day and night, they journey in flight.
My parents, my kin, my guiding light,
Why send me away from your side, out of sight?

When will normalcy return to light?
So I can stop recounting this unjust fight.

STRIKE THE DRUM (击鼓)

The war drums beat with a resounding blast,
Soldiers practice, their training steadfast.
Some build roads, walls strong and vast,
I alone march southward, with a heart full of contrast.

Following General Sunzi with dedication unsurpassed,
Resolving the Chen and Song feud at long last.
The battles are over, but my worries hold me fast,
My heart remains troubled, my thoughts outlast.

Where shall I live, where shall I reside?
My horse, oh where has it gone to hide?
How can I find my horse, my pride?
Deep in the forest, beneath the trees so wide.

"Life and death, never to part," we said by each other's
side,
Our promise cherished, our hearts full of pride.
I held your hand tightly, with love bona fide,
Together we'd stay, in life's endless ride.

Alas, the distance is impossibly wide,
We cannot meet, though in love we confide.
Alas, the separation, how long it's implied,
My heartfelt promise, I can't set aside.

TRIUMPHANT WIND (凯风)

The gentle breeze from the southern land,
Caresses the tender buds on the tree so grand.
The heart of the mulberry tree, firm and unplanned,
My mother raising children, the work well at hand.

The warm breeze from the southern land,
Turns mulberry trees into logs, it's all so grand.
My mother, wise and gentle, you understand,
Though I'm not good, I hold no reprimand.

Cold springs flow, a chill seeps through,
Near the source, by Jun County, true.
My mother raised seven, and it's her due,
I grew up, a burden, no thank you.

Yellowhammers sing in a melodious queue,
Their voices delightful, like morning dew.
My mother raised seven, and it's undue,
I worry my mother, as I misconstrue.

COCK PHEASANT (雄雉)

The male pheasant soars in the sky,
Stretching its wings, colors up high.
I miss my husband with a sigh,
Bringing sadness to me, oh my!

The male pheasant soars in the sky,
Up and down, with a sonorous cry.
My honest husband, I rely,
He truly makes my heart strain and sigh.

Watching the sun and moon in the sky,
Endless longing as time passes by.
The road between us, vast and high,
When, my husband, will you come by?

These gentlemen in high places, why,
Don't they know my husband's virtues, oh my!
He doesn't covet fame, nor wealth untie,
Yet he's beset by misfortune, oh why!

BITTER GOURD LEAVES (匏有苦叶)

The gourd leaves wither, the gourds ripe and prime,
The Ji River runs deep, no longer a climb.
When waters are deep, use a gourd for a ride,
When shallow, roll your pants up, stride by its side.

The Ji River swells, flooding far and wide,
A female pheasant cries by the waterside.
The waters are deep, over the wheel hubs they slide,
The female pheasant cries, seeking her guide.

Great geese in the sky with a sonorous glide,
The rising sun tints the east far and wide.
If you seek to wed, with the river's flow as your guide,
Do it now, while the river's ice is beside.

Boatman calls to ferry, the river's our pride,
Others cross first, I'll wait by your side.
Others cross first, but I'm here, don't chide,
I'll wait for my brother, let him not be denied.

VALLEY WIND (谷风)

A gust of wind rushes down the slope,
Dark clouds gather, pouring rain to cope.
Husband and wife should encourage hope,
Shouldn't they avoid anger, learning to mope?

Harvesting turnips and radishes in a row,
Must we want leaves and not roots, you know?
Don't cast away words of love we bestowed,
"To death, with you, I'll never go," we vowed.

Stepping out the door, I go slow,
My feet shuffle, reluctant to let go.
Not seeking distance, but closeness to show,
Who knew you'd only escort me to the door?

Who says bitter greens taste harsh, although,
I find them sweet as jicama in my flow.
You newlyweds, so joyous in your glow,
Siblings can't compare, this much I know.

Wei River joins Jing, where waters flow,
Jing's water may be muddy, Wei's pure, although.
You newlyweds, so blissful in your row,
I wonder if you've considered my woe?

Don't come to my fish dam, bestow,
Don't open my fish trap, let it go.
Now that you've made me your number zero,
Who will heed my plight and my sorrow?

Like fording a river where waters grow,
Use a raft or a boat where you go.
Or when waters are shallow, not a hefty tow,

I'll swim across, to the other side I'll show.

With this abundance, provisions will grow,
I make sure to prepare for winter's snow.
You newlyweds, so happy in your throw,
Using my things to block poverty's blow.

Rough voices, harsh words, unkind and low,
Heavy burdens I carry, it's tough, you know.
Back then, fearing poverty, our love did flow,
Now you avoid me like an unwanted crow.

DECLINE (式微)

It's dark, oh, it's dark, why so late?
Not for the king, but why night's fate?
It's not for the king; don't make me wait,
Will the night's dew dampen my attire's state?

It's dark, oh, it's dark, why this fate?
Not for the king; don't linger so late.
It's not for the king; don't close the gate,
Why tread on muddy paths, I contemplate?

MAOQIU (旄丘)

Oh, the vines on Maoqiu's mound,
Why do they stretch out so long?
Uncles and cousins from Wei's ground,
Why is it that they've been gone so long?

Why do they stay in their homes all day?
Surely, they must be waiting on their way.
Why do they wait for such a long delay?
There must be some reason, I would say.

Dressed in fur, warm and snug,
Riding a carriage, but not to the east they lug.
Uncles and cousins from Wei's land,
You don't seem to understand.

We are humble, small, and weak,
Lost and helpless, our future looks bleak.
Uncles and cousins from Wei's land,
Pretending not to know, it's what you speak.

JIAN XI (简兮)

Drums resound with a thunderous roar,
A grand dance performance, the center stage's core.
Under the sun's bright rays they explore,
Dance leaders in line, they take the floor.

Strong and vigorous, the dancers' core,
In the court, they dance and implore.
Their movements powerful, like a mighty boar,
Grips the reins like silk, without a sore.

Left hand holds a flute to explore,
Right hand waves a pheasant feather galore.
Their faces flushed red, like a brilliant ore,
The duke exclaims, "Quick, give them more!"

On high mountains, hazel trees galore,
In low fields, sorrel's green to adore.
Who is it in my heart that I'm waiting for?
The Western dance leader, strong to the core.

That handsome and gallant man I implore,
He hails from the Western land, I'm sure!

SPRING WATER (泉水)

Spring water gushes endlessly,
Returning to the Qi River, where it's meant to be.
Thinking of my homeland, Wei,
Not a day goes by without a sigh.

With my Ji family sisters, by and by,
I consult them, and together we try.
Thinking back to the farewell day,
Feasting in Mi County before I went away.

Women marrying into a foreign land's array,
Leaving parents and siblings, they say.
Before departing, I bid my aunt's display,
Along with my dear sisters, on that dismayed day.

If we could return and in Gan stay,
The place where we feasted before our foray.
Greasing the wheel's axles on display,
We'd gallop home in joy, no dismay.

Racing home quickly, what could go astray?
No trouble or misfortune to portray.
My thoughts to Fei's spring water obey,
Sighing constantly, without delay.

Thinking of Shucheng and Caoyi's array,
My sorrow and grief have no sway.
Driving the carriage for leisure each day,
To alleviate my worries, it's my forte.

NORTH GATE (北门)

Through the city's north gate, I tread,
Anxiety and troubles weigh on my head.
Lacking extravagance, poor is my spread,
Who knows the hardships I've been led?

Let it go!
It's heaven's plan, I dread,
What can I do, but move ahead?

Royal tasks are piled on my stead,
All governmental matters in my thread.
After a day's toil, returning to homestead,
Family's reproach fills me with dread.

Let it go!
It's heaven's plan, widespread,
In this matter, I have no thread.

Royal tasks burden me instead,
All governance rests on my head.
Returning home, I hear words widespread,
Mocking me as a fool, they've said.

Let it go!
It's heaven's plan, not just in my stead,
In this matter, I've no rebuttal to spread.

NORTH WIND (北风)

The north wind blows with icy might,
Heavy snow blankets in pure white.
My good friends, I invite,
To escape together, it's only right.

Why hesitate, walking slow in this plight?
Urgent matters press, trouble's in sight!

The world is full of sly and contrite,
But my friends and I will take flight.
Why hesitate, walking slow in this plight?
Urgent matters press, trouble's in sight!

All foxes' fur may be red and bright,
All crows may be black as night.
But my friends, let's unite,
Escape together and see the light.

Why hesitate, walking slow in this plight?
Urgent matters press, don't let it bite!

JING GIRL (静女)

A quiet maiden, so fair to see,
Invited me up to the tower, did she.
She hid from me with glee,
Leaving me searching helplessly.

A quiet maiden, so lovely to be,
Gave me a red grass reed willingly.
The reed is bright, as you can agree,
I cherish its color, so bold and free.

In the outskirts, where flowers flow endlessly,
A beauty gave me tithymalus to see.
Not the tithymalus, but it's she,
Who is beautiful as can be.

XIN TAI (新台)

Xin Tai, so bright and splendid,
The river flows east, unended.
I thought to marry a charming gent,
But he's as ugly as a frog, to my lament!

Xin Tai, tall and magnificent,
The river flows endlessly, so prominent.
I thought to marry a charming gent,
But he's unattractive, not elegant!

I cast my fishing net to catch some fish,
But to my surprise, a frog is my wish.
I thought to marry a charming gent,
But this man is so ugly, it's quite a glitch!

ER ZI CHENG ZHOU (二子乘舟)

Two people aboard a single leafy boat,
Gradually drifting further afloat.
Deeply missing you both, I devote,
My heart is filled with sorrow, remote.

Two people aboard a small boat, we gloat,
Gradually venturing far, with hope to denote.
Deeply missing you both, I wrote,
May you both have a safe and pleasant boat.

YONG FENG (鄘风)

"Yong Feng" is a popular musical tune from the Yong region. Yong was located in what is now Jixian County, Henan. After King Wu defeated the Shang dynasty, he took control of the area around the capital, Chaoge, and divided it into the three states of Bei, Yong, and Wei. Following King Wu's death, his younger brother Kang Shu was given control of the Yong region, creating the state of Wei. Consequently, the poems of "Yong Feng" are considered Wei poems. Notably, one of the poems, "Zai Chi," explicitly mentions its author, who was the first female poet in Chinese history, Lady Xumu. There are ten poems preserved from this tune.

BO ZHOU (柏舟)

The cypress wood boat is drifting along,
Drifting and floating in the middle of the river so strong.
With hair hanging low, a young man strong,
He's the one I have set my heart upon.

Until death, my feelings for him won't go wrong,
My heavens! My mother! Why don't you belong?

The cypress wood boat is drifting along,
Drifting ashore, where the river's banks throng.
With hair hanging low, a young man strong,
I wish to be with him, it's where I belong.

Until death, my feelings for him won't be wrong,
My heavens! My mother! Why don't you prolong?

QIANG YOU CI (墙有茨)

On the wall, there are thorns, oh, so sharp,
Do not remove them, hold them firm, don't hark.
Secrets from the palace, in the dark,
Must not spread, that's the mark.

If they do, it's a scandalous spark,
Ugly tales, whispered, and a remark.

JUN ZI XIE LAO (君子偕老)

She and the gentleman together will grow old,
With a jade hairpin and graceful stride, I'm told.
Graceful and composed, in manners untold,
Steady as a mountain, yet like flowing waters, they bide,
In well-fitting robes, adorned with colors that glow.
But her behavior is improper, I confide,
How can she be considered good by my side?

WEN CAI HUA MEI (文采华美)

Elegance and beauty, radiant and bright,
With adorned robes, a stunning sight.
Black hair, as dense as a moonless night,
No need for wigs to make it right.
Beside her temples, delicate pins ignite,
Like ivory combs, they hold hair tight.
Her complexion fair, her radiance might,
Could it be a celestial in plain sight?
Could it be a goddess descended with light?

Elegance and beauty, colors so bright,
Pure white garments, a dazzling invite.
Outside, they're of silk, a sheer delight,
Underneath, hemp garments, fittingly tight.
Her bright eyes so clear, they ignite,
Her brows and gaze, a lovely sprite.
Such beauty, could it be right?
A matchless beauty, truly a sight!

SANG ZHONG (桑中)

Where should I go to gather maidenhair fern?
To Wei's Meixiang, it's my concern.
Whose face is it that I yearn?
The lovely maiden named Jiang, in my discern.

She invited me to wait, and I did adjourn,
Inviting me to meet in the upper palace's return,
Sending me far, to the banks of Qi's churn.

Where should I go to gather wheat ears, my friend?
To Wei's Meixiang, to the north, we'll ascend.
Whose face is it that I yearn to attend?
The lovely maiden named Yi, my heart's amend.

She invited me to wait, and I did comprehend,
Inviting me to meet in the upper palace's blend,
Sending me far, to Qi's waters, we'll transcend.

Where should I go to gather turnips in the end?
To Wei's Meixiang, eastward, let's not offend.
Whose face is it that I yearn to defend?
The lovely maiden named Yong, to commend.

She invited me to wait, and I did intend,
Inviting me to meet in the upper palace's trend,
Sending me far, to Qi's waters, we'll blend.

CHUN ZHI BEN BEN (鹑之奔奔)

Quails fly in pairs, as do magpies with grace,
Yet this man shows no kindness, a heartless case.
Why do you regard him as your elder brother's face?

Magpies fly in pairs, quails take to the sky,
Yet this man lacks a conscience, oh my, oh my!
Why make him the ruler, oh, tell me why?

DING ZHI FANG ZHONG (定之方中)

The Pole Star shines in the middle of the sky,
Chuqiu's ancestral temple starts to rise up high.
Using the sun's shadow to determine and comply,
We lay the foundation for our homes, oh so spry.

Planting hazelnuts, chestnuts that will apply,
And trees for zither and se, oh my, oh my!
When they grow, they'll be instruments to try.

Standing on Qiu Hill, a panoramic view nearby,
Looking at Chuqiu and Tangyi, oh my, oh my!
Also Gaoyu and Shangan, fields of mulberry dye.
Observing from below, the fields of mulberry's dye,
The divination results are favorable, don't deny.
A bright future ahead, with hopes reaching high.

Gentle rain has just fallen from the sky,
Commanding the carriage and the little horses nigh.
Under a starry sky, we'll drive by and by,
With a whip, we'll stop at the mulberry to apply.

Not only for the people, but I'll also rely,
On my honest heart and far-reaching try.
To raise a warhorse, up to three thousand, oh my!

DI ZHI (蝃蝀)

A rainbow emerges in the eastern sky,
But no one dares to point a finger high.
When a maiden matures, she'll say goodbye,
Leaving her parents and siblings, oh so sly.

A rainbow emerges in the western sky,
In the morning, surely rain is nigh.
When a maiden matures, she'll say goodbye,
Leaving her parents and brothers, no lie.

But this person before us, oh my, oh my,
Doesn't follow the path, oh so spry.
No faith, no chastity, it's all awry,
Parents' teachings ignored, oh so wry.

XIANG SHU (相鼠)

Look at that rat, it still has fur,
As a human, how can you lack decor?
As a person, if you have no honor,
You might as well leave this world, for sure.

Look at that rat, it still has teeth,
As a person, no restraint, that's beneath.
As a human, if you lack belief,
Why delay? Depart, there's no relief.

Look at that rat, it still has a body,
As a person, behavior without dignity.
As a human, if you disregard courtesy,
Hurry, go die without hesitation, audacity.

GAN MAO (干旄)

The flag with ox tails soars high and wide,
People and horses reach the cityside.
Fine silk bound meticulously, they ride,
Four good horses, a gift for the stride.

Which virtuous gentleman did you decide,
To honor in such a way, with pride?
The one who advised, what did he provide?

The flag with eagle feathers, flying with pride,
People and horses approach the citywide.
Fine silk bound meticulously, they stride,
Five good horses, in favor, they confide.

Which virtuous gentleman did you decide,
To honor in such a way, where equestrians glide?
The one who advised, what will he betide?

The flag with bird feathers, soaring, they abide,
People and horses arrive, their strength implied.
Fine silk bound meticulously, they've complied,
Six good horses, they provide, bona fide.

Which virtuous gentleman did you decide,
To honor in such a way, their nobleness supplied?
The one who advised, what will he preside?

ZAI CHI (載馳)

Carriages and horses swiftly move ahead,
Returning to the homeland, to comfort our lord.
Driving the horses, the journey is long,
Wishing to arrive at Cao's place before long.
Xu's officials came to advise and implore,
Their decisions caused me to worry even more.
Even if you all disagree with my course,
I cannot return to the city, of course.

It seems your strategies are somewhat off course,
But my plan can still bear the course.
Even if you all disagree with my course,
I will never turn back, I assure.

It seems your strategies are somewhat off course,
But my thoughts can still hold discourse.
Climbing that high hill with no remorse,
Gathering seashells to ease my remorse.

Though women often tend to be verbose,
They have their own logic and own source.
Xu's officials reprimanded me, their force,
Truly, it was childish and off course.

Walking through the fields of our homeland's source,
The wheat stalks green, their growth on course.
Hurry, ask the great state for their endorse,
Relying on them to save us, of course.

All you gentlemen, please heed my discourse,
My plan is not mistaken, of course.
Though you all have many plans to endorse,
It's better for me to ask the great state, of course.

WEI FENG (卫风)

The "Wei Feng" also originated from the ancient Yin and Shang dynasty area, with content similar to the "Bei Feng" and "Yong Feng." Among the poems, "Shuo Ren" describes character images, and "Meng" portrays the characters' psychology, both of which have had a significant influence on later generations. There are ten extant poems in this category.

QI AO (淇奧)

Gazing at the winding bends of the Qi River's shore,
Green bamboo thrives, the banks adorned once more.
A gentleman of literary grace, so splendid in core,
Like ivory finely carved and jade forevermore.
Dignified and strong, his countenance to explore,
Gallant and bright-hearted, his spirit to implore.
A gentleman of literary grace, forever we adore,
In our hearts, his memory we will ever restore.

Gazing at the winding bends of the Qi River's shore,
Lush green bamboo, its branches, rich and more.
A gentleman of literary grace, shining as before,
Like starry jade, his splendor we can't ignore.
His hat adorned with a single gem's galore,
Dignified and bold, his heart's wide open door.
A gentleman of literary grace, forever we explore,
In our hearts, his memory we will ever store.

Gazing at the winding bends of the Qi River's shore,
Lush green bamboo thrives, lush as evermore.
A gentleman of literary grace, a treasure to restore,
Like gold and silver, qualities he did outpour.
Like jade and precious stones, virtues he bore,
Broad, gentle, and warm, his presence we implore.
A gentleman of literary grace, forever to adore,
In our hearts, his memory we will evermore.

KAO PAN (考槃)

Built a wooden house amid the mountain's nook,
A virtuous person dwells there, like an open book.
Sleeps alone, awakens alone, and silently brooks,
Happiness remembered without a word, it's shook.

Built a wooden house upon the hill's outlook,
A virtuous person resides, contented, unshook.
Sleeps alone, awakens alone, no reason to forsook,
This mountain abode, never to be mistook.

Built a wooden house on the highlands, outlook,
A virtuous person resides, in solitude he took.
Sleeps alone, awakens alone, a serene brook,
Here, joy cannot be spoken, only overlooked.

SHUO REN (硕人)

Tall and graceful, a beautiful woman there,
Adorned in silk and an outerwear so fair.
She's the beloved daughter of Qi's lord,
And the doting wife of Wei, by accord.
She's the prince's sister, close in blood,
Xing's lord's kin, a bond understood.
Tan Gong, her brother-in-law, it's declared.

Fingers slender like young sorrel leaves so fine,
Skin as fair as congealed fat, so divine.
Her neck's grace akin to a serpent's line,
Teeth like melon seeds, white in a line.
Her forehead square, brows arch like twine,
With a faint smile, dimples divine.
Her beautiful eyes, like stars that shine.

A tall and elegant figure she portrays,
Resting her carriage near the countryside's maze.
Four mighty horses, their spirit ablaze,
Red silk adorns their reins, a vibrant blaze.
Riding a feathered chariot, she starts her days,
Officials complete their morning praise,
To spare Lord Wei from toiling always.

The Yellow River's waters flow in endless spree,
Roaring as they rush toward the northern sea.
Fishing nets are cast, a roaring glee,
Fish splash into the nets, wild and free.
Reeds and grasses flourish, a verdant spree,
The Jiang family's daughters in finery,
Retainers robust and full of esprit.

MENG (氓)

A young lad walks, all smiles and glee,
Holding cloth coins, pretending to buy, you see.
But he's not here for silks, believe me,
Using this as pretext, a match to decree.
The day you crossed the Qi River with me,
Taking me to Dunqiu, then saying goodbye,
It wasn't my intent to mistake the plea,
You never sent a matchmaker, that's the decree.
Please don't hold a grudge, hear my plea,
Let's set the autumn season for our marquee.

Climbing the broken, shattered city wall,
Gazing toward Fuguan, yearning for your call.
Through my eyes, I cannot see it all,
Anxiously, my heart tears, a waterfall.
Now that you return from the city's thrall,
You speak and smile, no sorrows befall.
You've prayed and sought, heard the call,
The divination showed no ill, that's the ball.
Quickly, with your horse-drawn carriage, haul,
Bring my dowry, the nuptial enthrall.

When mulberry leaves are still so green,
Lush and moist, a vibrant scene.
Oh, little spotted dove, let it be seen,
Don't feast on mulberries, let them convene.
Young ladies, heed these words, don't lean,
Too much on men, keep your self-esteem.
If men become attached, it's been seen,
When you say it's over, hold your sheen.
If women get attached, it's extreme,
Forever in their hearts, it's a dream.

Now the mulberry leaves have turned so dry,
Yellowed, withered, they flutter and fly.
Since I came to your home, oh my,
Many years of hardship, oh my!
The Qi River surged, bidding goodbye,
Splashing my carriage, oh my!
As a wife, I've done naught awry,
But your actions are contrary, oh my!
Inconstant, no rules, oh my,
Inconsistent behavior, oh my!

For years married, a dutiful wife, oh my,
Managing all affairs, no strife, oh my.
Early to rise, late to sleep, no lie, oh my,
Working tirelessly, never saying goodbye.
Your wishes fulfilled, reaching the sky, oh my,
Turning cruel and making me cry, oh my.
Your brothers know not, oh my,
Seeing me return, they laugh and imply.
Upon reflection, thoughts multiply,
Only I bear the hurt, oh my.

Back then, you said, "Together we'll die,"
Growing old together, my heart's sigh.
Though the Qi River is wide, it has a tie,
Though marshes are vast, they're not a lie, oh my.
Recalling our innocent days, oh my,
Laughing and joking, joy up high.
Promises made, oh my,
Never thought you'd change, oh my.
All vows, oh my,
From this point on, separate lives, oh my.

ZHU GAN (竹竿)

A fishing rod so slim and long,
Once used to fish in the Qi River's song.
Don't you ever think of where you belong,
The journey is long; it's hard to prolong.

The spring source flows on the left so strong,
The Qi River flows on the right so long.
For young girls, marriage means moving along,
Away from parents and brothers, headstrong.

The Qi River flows on the right so long,
The spring source on the left, the journey's throng.
With a slight smile and jade-like teeth, so strong,
Adorning with jade, jingling a melodious song.

The Qi River flows on, waters meander and throng,
Cypress oars and pine boats float along.
I'll go on a journey to quell my disheartening,
To ease my homesickness and stop its torment.

WAN LAN (芄兰)

On the Wan Lan branch, they form a pair,
A young lad wears a horn ornament with care.
Though he wears a horn ornament, beware,
For it doesn't suit me, this is my declare.
When he walks, he's slow, takes his time to bear,
Swaying side to side, a wide belt to wear.

On the Wan Lan branch, leaves curl and share,
A young lad wears an armband, do you dare?
Though he wears an armband, don't think we pair,
He doesn't draw near; he seems unaware.
When he walks, he's slow, takes his time to bear,
Swaying side to side, a wide belt to wear.

HE GUANG (河广)

Who says the Yellow River's broad and vast?
A small reed raft can travel it so fast.
Who says Song is distant, unsurpassed?
Lift your heels high, and it's seen at last.

Who says the Yellow River's wide and vast?
Too narrow for a small wooden boat to pass.
Who says Song is distant, it's in contrast?
One morning's journey, the distance can't amass.

BO XI (伯兮)

My husband, so valiant and bold,
His talents and wisdom, a sight to behold.
A spear, twenty feet long, in his hand he'd hold,
Leading the way, as a king, he'd be extolled.

Since my husband left for the eastern war,
My hair has scattered, like drifting spore.
Could there be no hair oil in the store?
For whom should I beautify anymore?

I long for a great rain to pour,
But the sun shines bright, what's more.
Every day, I await him at my door,
Though it pains my head, my heart is pure.

Where can I find the Forget-Worry herb's spore?
I'll plant it here, near my floor.
Every day, I think of him, that's for sure,
His memory lingers, my heart's deplore.

YOU HU (有狐)

A fox, slowly and leisurely,
Strolls upon the Qi River's bridge so free.
In my heart, there's such worry,
You're without clothes, it's easy to see.

A fox, slowly and leisurely,
On the shallow riverbank, there you be.
In my heart, there's such worry,
Without a belt, it's not as it should be.

A fox, slowly and leisurely,
By the river's edge, so carelessly.
In my heart, there's such worry,
You're without clothes, my heart's in misery.

MU GUA (木瓜)

Gift me a wooden pear with grace,
In return, I'll offer jade in its place.
Not just for gratitude, you I embrace,
This signifies my love, an eternal embrace.

Gift me a wooden peach, replace,
With precious jade, in this case.
Not merely in response, a surface trace,
It symbolizes a lasting bond we'll chase.

Gift me a wooden plum, encase,
With jewel-like jade, our love's base.
Not just in response, a mere surface lace,
I want us to be together, in any case.

SHU LI (黍离)

Look at the foxtail millet in rows so fine,
And the sorghum stalks as they intertwine.
I take a step forward, then I recline,
In my heart, only worries and woes align.
Those who know me, they opine,
That my heart is heavy, they assign.
Those who don't know me, in decline,
They think I'm seeking, in a straight line.
High above in the sky, the divine,
Who's causing me to leave home, malign?

Look at the foxtail millet in rows so long,
And the sorghum ears, crimson strong.
I take a step forward, then I'm gone,
Like someone who's had too much to throng.
Those who know me, they can't be wrong,
My heart is heavy, like a solemn song.
Those who don't know me, they prolong,
Thinking I'm in pursuit, for what's lifelong.
High above in the sky, so strong,
Who's causing me to leave home, so wrong?

Look at the foxtail millet in rows so bright,
And the sorghum ears, a crimson light.
I take a step forward, then I'm in flight,
My heart aches as if it's choked up tight.
Those who know me, they understand my plight,
My heart is heavy, a sleepless night.
Those who don't know me, they might,
Think I'm seeking something, out of sight.
High above in the sky, shining bright,
Who's causing me to leave home, in the night?

A GENTLEMAN'S SERVICE (君子于役)

A husband serves in distant lands,
The duration uncertain,
I know not where he's gone.
The roosters have returned to their coops,
The sun has set in the west,
Herds of cattle and sheep descend the slopes.
My husband serves in a distant place,
How can I not miss him?

A husband serves in distant lands,
Days and months seem endlessly long,
I know not when we'll gather again.
The roosters are roosting,
The sun is slowly setting in the west,
Herds of cattle and sheep return home.
My husband serves in a distant place,
I hope he won't go hungry.

A GENTLEMAN RADIANT AND JOYFUL (君子阳阳)

My husband is joyous and radiant,
In his left hand, he holds many reeds,
With his right hand, he beckons me to dance in the room.
We are delighted, our hearts are carefree.

My husband is content and cheerful,
In his left hand, he wields feathers in dance,
With his right hand, he beckons me to frolic.
Our spirits are soaring high.

YANGZI WATERS (扬之水)

The small river flows with gentle ripples,
Unable to carry a bundle of firewood.
The person I long for in my heart,
Did not stay with me to defend our homeland.
Day and night, I yearn,
When will I return to my homeland?

The small river flows with gentle ripples,
Unable to carry a bundle of reeds.
The person I long for in my heart,
Did not stay with me to guard our borders.
Day and night, I yearn,
When will I return to my homeland?

The small river flows with gentle ripples,
Unable to carry a bundle of bulrushes.
The person I long for in my heart,
Did not stay with me to protect our land.
Day and night, I yearn,
When will I return to my homeland?

IN THE MIDST OF THE VALLEY, THERE IS SHEPHERD'S PURSE (中谷有蓷)

The shepherd's purse vines stretch long and far,
Climbing up to the wetlands by the river.
Far from family and brothers,
I call others "father" in their face.
Even if I call them "father" repeatedly,
They won't show me any care.

The shepherd's purse vines stretch long and far,
Climbing up to the dry land by the riverbank.
Far from family and brothers,
I call others "mother" in their face.
Even if I call them "mother" countless times,
They won't treat me like a son.

The shepherd's purse vines stretch long and far,
Climbing up to the wetlands by the river.
Far from family and brothers,
I call others "older brother" in their face.
Even if I call them "older brother" every day,
They won't respond.

PICKING REED LEAVES (采葛)

The one who picks reed leaves,
I haven't seen her for a day,
It feels like it's been three months!

The one who picks slender reeds,
I haven't seen her for a day,
It feels like it's been three autumns!

The one who picks wormwood leaves,
I haven't seen her for a day,
It feels like it's been three years!

BIG CART (大车)

The big cart rolls along with a clatter,
Green woolen robes flutter like reeds.
Could it be that I don't miss you?
In love, I fear you might not dare.

The big cart moves forward with a clang,
Red woolen robes gleam like jewels.
Could it be that I don't miss you?
Afraid you won't elope with me.

Living apart in separate rooms,
In death, we'll share a single grave.
You don't believe what I say,
Let the sun bear witness to our love.

Hemp in the Hillock (丘中有麻)

In the hemp field on the hillside,
I await the young lad Liu Zijie.
That young lad Liu Zijie,
I hope he comes to assist me.

In the wheat field on the slope,
I await the young lad Liu Ziguo.
That young lad Liu Ziguo,
I hope he comes to dine at my home.

Under the plum trees on the hill,
Young Liu has arrived.
That young lad surnamed Liu,
Gifts me a jade pendant to express his feelings.

ZHENG FENG (郑风)

    Zheng refers to the name of a state. During the reign of King Xuan of the Western Zhou Dynasty, his brother Ji You was granted land in Zheng (present-day Huazhou in Shaanxi), becoming Duke Huan of Zheng. At the end of King You's reign, the Quanrong tribe killed both King You and Duke Huan. Duke Huan's son, Juetu, succeeded him, known as Duke Wu. The state continued to be called "Zheng," and its capital was in present-day Xinzheng, Henan. "Zheng FENG " comprises poems from after Duke Wu of Zheng established the state, and they are all works from the Eastern Zhou period, totaling twenty-one poems, mostly focused on love and relationships.

DARK ROBES (緇衣)

Black official robes fit so well,
Worn out, I'll make you a new set.
Wear them to the government office,
When you return, I'll have new attire ready for you.

Black official robes look so good,
Worn out, I'll make alterations for you.
Wear them to the government office,
When you return, I'll have new attire ready for you.

Black official robes, so roomy and loose,
Worn out, I'll redesign them for you.
Wear them to the government office,
When you return, I'll have new attire ready for you.

JIANG ZHONGZI (将仲子)

Younger brother Zhongzi, listen to me,
Don't step over the inner and outer walls.
Don't let the branches of the jujube tree hurt you.
It's not that I cherish these trees,
It's because I fear my parents.
I'm constantly worried about you, my brother,
And I'm afraid our parents will scold me.
This matter truly makes me anxious.

Younger brother Zhongzi, listen to me,
Don't climb over the walls of our house.
Don't disturb the mulberry trees by the wall.
It's not that I cherish these trees,
It's because I fear our elder brother will stop you.
I'm constantly worried about you, my brother,
And I'm afraid our elder brother will scold me.
This matter truly makes me anxious.

Younger brother Zhongzi, listen to me,
Don't trespass into our backyard.
Don't let the branches of the sandalwood tree hurt you.
It's not that I cherish these trees,
It's because I fear others will gossip.
I'm constantly worried about you, my brother,
Idle talk can harm a person,
This matter truly makes me anxious.

SHU IN THE FIELD (叔于田)

Uncle goes hunting and leaves the house,
The lanes seem deserted as if no one lives here.
Could it be true that no one lives here?
No one can compare to Uncle,
He's so handsome and kind.

My uncle goes hunting and leaves the house,
No one in the lanes is drinking.
Is it really the case that no one is drinking?
No one can compare to my uncle,
He's so handsome and refined.

My uncle rides a horse into the wilderness,
No one in the lanes knows how to ride.
Is it really the case that no one knows how to ride?
No one can surpass him,
He's indeed handsome and strong.

UNCLE IN THE FIELD (大叔于田)

Uncle goes hunting like going to war,
Driving a chariot with four horses moving forward.
Holding the reins like strands of silk,
Riding horses as if they were dancing in the air.
Uncle is amidst the lush grass,
Kindling a roaring hunting fire.
Shirtless, he confronts the tigers,
Bringing back prey to offer at the lord's house.
I advise Uncle not to be too careless,
Beware the fierce tigers that might harm you.

Uncle goes hunting like going to war,
Driving a chariot with yellow horses galloping ahead.
Two fine horses lead the way,
Two riding horses follow in formation like geese.
Uncle is amidst the lush grass,
The hunting fire burns even brighter.
Uncle's archery skills are superb,
His chariot handling is extraordinary.
At times he reins in the galloping horses,
At times he lets them freely run.

Uncle goes hunting like going to war,
Driving a variegated horse-drawn carriage that never
stops.
In the center, fine horses advance in line,
The riding horses seem to move on their own.
Uncle is amidst the lush grass,
The hunting fire roars fiercely.
Uncle's steeds gradually slow down,
His archery becomes infrequent.
He opens the quiver, places the arrows,
And stows away the bow in its case.

QING PEOPLE (清人)

The Qingyi army is stationed in Pengcheng,
Mounted soldiers in armor, truly imposing.
Adorned with jade and precious gems on their two spears,
By the Yellow River, it seems like a leisurely courtyard.

The Qingyi army is stationed in Xiao,
Mounted soldiers in armor, proud and bold.
Adorned with pheasant feathers on their two spears,
By the Yellow River, they roam freely.

The Qingyi army is stationed in Zhou,
Mounted soldiers in armor, racing onward.
Turning left and drawing their swords to the right,
In the army, they seem well-prepared.

LAMB'S FUR (羔裘)

Wearing a lamb's fur coat, glossy and sleek,
A person who is upright and fine.
Just such a person,
Unafraid to sacrifice for the lord's labor.

Wearing a leopard-trimmed lamb's fur robe,
Tall and strong, a person of grandeur.
Just such a person,
Fitting to be a high-ranking official of the country.

The lamb's fur coat is truly splendid,
Adorned with fine silk, even more radiant.
Just such a person,
An outstanding choice for the nation.

FOLLOWING THE MAIN ROAD (遵大路)

Walking along the main road with you,
Holding onto your sleeve tightly.
Please don't dislike me,
Don't forget our old affection.

Walking along the main road with you,
Closely gripping your hand.
Please don't mind my homely appearance,
Don't forget our years of love.

WOMAN SAYS THE ROOSTER CROWS
(女曰鸡鸣)

The woman says, "The rooster has crowed."
The man says, "The day is about to break."
"You should quickly get up and see the sky,
The morning star is shining brightly."
"The birds are flying in the sky,
Shoot some ducks and geese for you to taste."

"Shoot down ducks and geese, bring them home,
Cook them into delicious dishes, so fragrant.
Enjoy the meal with some wine,
Our loving life will last a hundred years.
You play the zither, and I'll beat the se,
As a husband and wife, we'll live in happiness."

"I know you truly care for me,
So, I give you a jade pendant to express my love.
I know you're gentle and tender with me,
So, I give you a jade pendant to express my affection.
I know you deeply love me,
So, I give you a jade pendant to express my heart."

TRAVELING WITH A MAIDEN (有女同车)

A maiden and I travel together in a carriage,
Her appearance is like a blooming flower.
Her figure is graceful as a bird in flight,
Adorned with precious jade, she shines brightly.
She's the beautiful maiden named Jiang,
Her demeanor is elegant and dignified.

A maiden and I journey on the same path,
Her countenance is like a hibiscus flower.
Her figure is light as a bird in the sky,
The sound of her jade ornaments is melodious.
The beautiful maiden, her surname is Jiang,
Her fine reputation is unforgettable.

FUSANG TREES ON THE MOUNTAIN
(山有扶苏)

On the mountain, Fusang branches are lush,
In the wetlands, lotus flowers bloom in red.
What I see is not a handsome man,
But you, this foolish and crazy lad.

On the mountain, tall pine trees grow,
In the wetlands, horsetails burst forth in crimson.
What I see is not a handsome man,
But you, this slick and crafty boy.

FALLING LEAVES (莈兮)

Falling leaves, oh, they drift downward,
Autumn winds blow, gently they sway.
All you cheerful young lads here,
I'll start the song, and you follow the tune.

Falling leaves, oh, they drift downward,
Autumn winds blow, gently they sway.
All you joyful young lads here,
I'll start the song, and you join in.

THE SLY LAD (狡童)

That lovely young lad,
Why won't you speak to me?
Because of you,
I can't even eat my meal.

That lovely young lad,
Why won't you dine with me?
Because of you,
I can't sleep peacefully.

LIFTING THE SKIRTS (褰裳)

If you love me and miss me,
Quickly lift your skirt and wade across the Zhen River.
If you no longer love me,
Are there no other young men coming for me?
You silly, silly boy!

If you love me and miss me,
Quickly lift your skirt and wade across the Wei River.
If you no longer love me,
Aren't there other young men around?
You silly, silly boy!

The Handsome Man (丰)

Hard to forget your splendid appearance,
You waited for a long time in the alley.
Regret not walking with you.

Hard to forget your robust physique,
You waited for a long time in the hall.
Regret not going with you.

Wearing satin clothes on your body,
Covered with an embroidered robe outside.
Uncles and brothers, hurry to come,
Drive a carriage to pick me up and return together.

Covered with an embroidered robe outside,
Wearing satin clothes inside.
Uncles and brothers, hurry to come,
Drive a carriage to pick me up and return together!

EAST GATE MARKETPLACE (东门之墠)

Outside the east gate, it's quite spacious,
Madder grass grows on the hillside.
Your home is so close to mine,
Yet it feels like you're far away.

Under the chestnut trees outside the city's east gate,
There's a good household to be found.
Could it be that you don't miss me?
It would be foolish not to seek me out.

WIND AND RAIN (风雨)

Winds and rain mix, it's cold and dreary,
Roosters seek companions, crowing cheerily.
Finally, I see my husband return,
Anxious thoughts, why won't they cease?

Fierce winds and pouring rain, it's gloomy and bleak,
Roosters seek companions, crowing endlessly.
Finally, I see my husband return,
The ailment of longing, why won't it fade?

ZIJIN (子衿)

Your collar is green, oh, young man so fair,
My heart is heavy with constant care.
Even if I haven't come to find you,
Why haven't you sent me a message?

Wearing a green collar, oh, young man so fine,
In my heart, thoughts of you entwine.
Even if I haven't come to find you,
Why haven't you come to meet me?

Walking back and forth, so many trips we've made,
On the city gate tower, I've waited for days.
One day without seeing you feels as long
As three months that have passed.

YANG'S WATERS (扬之水)

The small river flows, so narrow and meandering,
A bundle of reeds can easily get stuck.
Originally, there were few siblings at home,
Only you and I, supporting each other.
Don't easily believe what others say,
They truly want to deceive you.

The small river flows, gently and slowly,
A bundle of firewood can't drift away.
Originally, there were few siblings at home,
Only the two of us, relying on each other.
Don't easily believe what others say,
They can't be trusted.

OUTSIDE THE EASTERN GATE (出其东门)

Outside the eastern gate,
There are countless young women.
Though they are numerous,
None are the one in my heart.
Wearing a white dress and green skirt,
Only then do you make me happy and close.

Outside the city gates,
There are numerous young women, like flowers.
Though they are abundant,
None are the one I love.
Wearing a white dress and a red headscarf,
Only then do you make me fond and joyful.

WILD CREEPERS (野有蔓草)

Wild creepers spread out, forming a carpet,
Dewdrops on the grass glisten and gleam.
A beautiful maiden walks along the road,
With delicate eyebrows and a charming look.
Meeting unexpectedly is such a delight,
Fulfilling my heart's desire just right.

Wild creepers spread out, covering the ground,
Dewdrops on the grass are large and round.
A beautiful maiden walks along the way,
With clear eyes and a lovely face.
Meeting unexpectedly is so fortunate,
Sharing a joyful moment, our hearts resonate.

ZHEN AND WEI RIVERS (溱洧)

The Zhen River and Wei River are long and winding,
River waters flow towards the distance.
Men and women from the city venture out,
Holding shepherd's purse for good fortune.
The maiden says, "Let's go take a look."
The young man says, "I've already been once."
"What's the harm in going again?"
By the Wei River, along the riverbank,
The place is lively and spacious.
Men and women stroll together,
Playfully, cheerfully,
Exchanging a peony flower as a keepsake.

The Zhen River and Wei River are long and winding,
River waters flow so clear and bright.
Men and women from the city venture out,
The crowd is bustling and clamorous.
The maiden says, "Let's go take a look."
The young man says, "I've already been once."
"What's the harm in going again?"
By the Wei River, along the riverbank,
The place is lively and spacious.
Men and women stroll together,
Playfully, joyfully,
Exchanging a peony flower, expressions linger.

QIN SONGS (齐风)

"Qin Songs" are the poems of the state of Qi. The territory of Qi was located in what is now the vicinity of Zibo in Shandong Province. After King Wu of Zhou conquered the Shang Dynasty, he enfeoffed the meritorious Jiàng Tàigōng in Qi, with its capital in Yingqiu (modern-day Linzi). This region was blessed with proximity to the sea, rich in fish and salt resources, which led to the people's extravagant customs. The poetry from this region has a soothing and elegant style. Qi was also surrounded by mountains, and its people were skilled in hunting, reflecting a martial spirit, which is evident in their poetry. Additionally, the poems touch on themes related to marriage, love, and the life of the aristocracy. Thus, Ji Zha praised the Qi Songs as "grand and magnificent" in his musical treatise, and the "Le Ji" (乐记) also says, "Those who are gentle yet decisive should sing the songs of Qi." Eleven poems from this state have survived.

THE CROWING OF THE ROOSTER (鸡鸣)

"You hear the rooster crowing,
And the ministers have gone to court."
"It's not the rooster crowing,
It's just the buzzing of a fly."

"You see the eastern sky brightening,
The court is filled with ministers."
"It's not the eastern sky brightening,
It's the moonlight shining."

"You hear the insects buzzing,
They are willing to enter your dreams with you."
"The court is filled with ministers returning home,
Please don't speak ill of me."

STILL (还)

Your hunting skills are truly excellent,
Meeting you in the hills and valleys is delightful.
Chasing after two wild boars on horseback,
You compliment my agility with a bow.

Your archery skills are truly superb,
Meeting you in the hilly terrain is enjoyable.
Pursuing two male boars side by side,
You praise my extraordinary technique.

Your physique is strong and your bearing is impressive,
Meeting you on the southern slope is exciting.
Chasing two wolves on horseback,
You commend my uncommon skills.

CLOTHES (著)

The bridegroom waits for me at the front gate,
His ears are adorned with white silk threads,
Decorated with radiant jade.

The bridegroom waits for me in the courtyard,
His ears are adorned with green silk cords,
With precious jewels shining brightly.

The bridegroom waits for me in the main hall,
His ears are adorned with golden silk threads,
With precious jewels emitting a brilliant glow.

EASTERN SUNLIGHT (东方之日)

The red sun rises in the east,
There's a beautiful maiden,
She enters my new chamber.
She enters my new chamber,
Following my footsteps.

The moon is rising in the east,
There's a beautiful maiden,
She enters my inner room.
She enters my inner room,
Following my footsteps.

BEFORE DAWN IN THE EAST (东方未明)

The east is still dark,
Frantically getting dressed, I'm in a hurry.
In my haste, I mix up my clothes,
All because the messenger is calling.

The east is not yet bright, the sky is black,
Putting on clothes in a hurry, I'm anxious.
In my anxiety, I mix up my clothes,
All because the messenger is shouting.

Building a fence, cutting willow branches,
The overseer stands nearby, glaring.
Unable to sleep on time,
Early to rise and late to rest, truly toilsome.

THE SOUTHERN MOUNTAIN (南山)

In the high, towering mountains of Qi,
A sturdy fox runs along behind.
The roads of Lu are wide and smooth,
It's here Lady Wenjiang married Lord of Lu.
Now that you've wedded Lord of Lu,
Why still yearn for your old love?

Two pairs of hemp shoes placed side by side,
Hat strings hanging down on either side.
The roads of Lu are wide and smooth,
Wenjiang set off on this journey.
Now that you're Lady of Lu,
Why let your old feelings linger?

How to cultivate hemp on the farm so well?
There's a method to tilling the land.
How to go about marrying a bride?
You must first seek your parents' consent.
Now that you've sought your parents' consent,
Why let her act so recklessly?

How to chop firewood, what's the trick?
Without an axe, it won't be done right.
How to go about marrying a bride?
It can't be done without a matchmaker.
Now that you've brought her into the home,
Why allow her to act so foolishly?

FUTIAN (甫田)

Don't cultivate that Futian land,
Where the wild grass grows abundantly.
Don't yearn for distant people,
Sorrow and distress will torment your heart.

Don't till the fields of Futian,
Endless wild grass is found there.
Don't think of distant people,
Your heart will be filled with sorrow and care.

In childhood, tender and charming,
Hair tied up like a pair of ram's horns.
When you see each other again later,
Suddenly don the hat of an adult.

LULING (卢令)

The hunting dog's collar bells jingle,
The hunter is gentle and handsome.

The hunting hound wears mother and child rings,
The hunter's long hair is curly and flowing.

The hunting hound wears two copper rings,
The hunter is robust and capable.

BIGOU (敝笱)

Broken traps placed at the fishing weir,
Failing to catch large fish like crucian carp.
Wenjiang returns to Qi to see her elder brother,
Accompanied by people as numerous as clouds.

Broken traps placed at the fishing weir,
Unable to capture big fish like pike and perch.
Wenjiang returns to Qi to see her elder brother,
Accompanied by people like a downpour.

Broken traps placed at the fishing weir,
Fish swim freely without hindrance.
Wenjiang returns to Qi to see her elder brother,
Accompanied by people like flowing water.

ZAIQU (载驱)

Horse-drawn carriages speed along with clattering wheels,
Bamboo curtains and red curtains are dazzling.
The roads of Lu are mostly level and smooth,
Wenjiang travels back and forth at all hours.

Four horses drive the carriage in perfect formation,
Reins loose as they gallop freely.
The roads of Lu are mostly level and smooth,
Wenjiang happily roams around.

The Wen River flows with rippling waves,
The road is bustling with people.
The roads of Qi are mostly level and smooth,
Wenjiang freely wanders here.

The Wen River's waters curl and surge,
People on the road are like watching tides.
The roads of Qi are mostly level and smooth,
Wenjiang moves about freely.

YIJI (猗嗟)

Your appearance is so beautiful,
Your figure is so slender.
Your forehead is so wide,
Beautiful eyes shimmer with radiance.
Your steps are agile and graceful,
Your archery skills are impressive.

Youthful and beautiful, full of sunlight,
Clear and bright are your eyes.
The rituals have been completed,
You shoot arrows into the target tirelessly.
Every arrow hits the bullseye,
Truly, my nephew is outstanding.

Young and handsome, truly lovely,
Clear and shining are your eyes.
Graceful and extraordinary in your dance,
Every arrow hits the mark.
Four consecutive shots, all in the center,
He can defend against enemies and rebellions.

WEI FENG (魏风)

"Wei Feng" consists of seven poems, all written during the early Spring and Autumn period. The ancient territory of Wei was located in the northeastern part of modern-day Ruicheng in Shanxi Province. The region was described as rugged and the people were known for their poverty, simplicity, and thriftiness. Consequently, Wei poetry often expresses the hardships of their lives and their discontent with the rulers. "Shuoshi" (硕鼠) and "Fat Tan" (伐檀) are notable works from this collection.

GE JU (葛屨)

Woven shoes made of wisteria vines,
How can they withstand the frosty ground?
Delicate and feeble are these hands,
How can they mend clothing so profound?
Sewing the waist and stitching the neckline,
For that beautiful lady to wear.

The lady displays arrogance,
Turning away and avoiding to the left,
An ivory hairpin adorns her head.
Indeed, her narrow-mindedness has no bounds,
A poem satirizing her is quite fitting.

FEN JU (汾沮洳)

By the banks of the Fen River's lowlands,
Picking tender and crispy vegetables with haste.
Who is that handsome young man,
So incredibly beautiful, difficult to appraise?
Incredibly beautiful, beyond comparison,
Far superior to the official's road.

By the banks of the Fen River's edge,
Picking mulberry leaves to feed silkworms.
Who is that handsome young man,
As beautiful as a blooming flower?
As beautiful as a blooming flower,
Far superior to the official's path.

By the bend of the Fen River's flow,
Harvesting wild rice with speed.
Who is that handsome young man,
As beautiful as jade?
As beautiful as jade,
Far superior to the official's clan.

YUAN YOU TAO (园有桃)

In the garden, there's a peach tree,
Its peaches make a fine dish to eat.
With inner sadness I have no place to express,
So I'll sing songs and rhymes, not less.
Those who don't understand me,
Said, "You are too proud, you see.
The other person is right, indeed,
What you say is not necessary."

With inner sadness I have no place to express,
Who truly understands my distress?
No one understands my distress,
I guess I'll stop thinking, no more, no less!

In the garden, there's a jujube tree,
Its jujubes provide a satisfying feast.
With inner sadness I have no place to express,
So I'll roam around, east and west.
Those who don't understand me,
Said, "You are deviating from the norm, you see.
The other person is right, indeed,
What you say is not necessary."

With inner sadness I have no place to express,
Who truly understands my distress?
No one understands my distress,
I guess I'll stop thinking, no more, no less!

ZHI HU (陟岵)

Climbing up the green hills covered in grass,
Climbing high, I look toward my father.
Father says, "Ah!
My child is serving far away,
Day and night, I worry incessantly.
Take care and stay safe,
Finish your service and come back early!"

Climbing up to the high, bald mountaintop,
Climbing to the summit, I look at my mother.
Mother says, "Ah!
My child is serving in a distant place,
Day and night, I think of you.
Be careful and stay safe,
Maintain your strength and return safely!"

Climbing up that high hillside,
Climbing up high, I look at my elder brother.
Brother says, "Ah!
Younger brother is serving far away,
Sooner or later, I will be with my companions.
Take care and stay safe,
Stay strong and return alive!"

WITHIN TEN ACRES (十亩之间)

Amidst ten acres of mulberry trees,
The mulberry-picking maiden is at ease.
Come, let's go home together, if you please.

Beyond ten acres in the mulberry grove,
Many maidens pick mulberries in troves.
Come, let's head back to our village, it behooves.

CUTTING SANDALWOOD (伐檀)

Clang, clang, the sound echoes, cutting sandalwood,
Chopped down and left by the riverbank, understood.
The river water flows clear, calmly it stood.
Without planting or harvesting, as idle as we could.
Why can't we collect enough grain as we should?
No hunting or capturing wild game in the wood.
Yet, boars and badgers hang in our neighborhood.
These lords and young masters, do they eat for good?

Clang, clang, cutting sandalwood for the chariot wheel,
Chopped down and left by the river, it's the deal.
The river water flows clear, as in a dream-like reel.
Without planting or harvesting, as if in a surreal.
Why does our granary always overfill and overspill?
No hunting or capturing game, yet we have a surplus still.
Quails and partridges hang in your courtyard, nil.
These lords and young masters, they must have their fill!

Clang, clang, cutting sandalwood for the wheel's core,
Chopped down and left by the river's shore.
The river water ripples gently, as told of yore.
Without planting or harvesting, our harvests are galore.
Why do we have such abundant grain, and more?
No hunting or capturing quails, a new score.
The lords and young masters, wealth they explore.
But why, for our toil and labor, do they ignore?

THE FAT MOUSE (硕鼠)

Oh, fat mouse, oh, fat mouse,
Don't steal my millet from the house.
For years, I've worked hard to feed you, no doubt.
But you don't care if I live or if I'm out.
I swear to leave you from this day forth,
To a better land, I'll head to the north.
A land of joy, an ideal worth,
A peaceful place to make my berth.

Oh, fat mouse, oh, fat mouse,
Don't steal my wheat or ransack my house.
For years, I've toiled to feed you, so douse.
Your ingratitude has left me to grouse.
I swear to leave you from this hour,
To a happier place, with newfound power.
A better life, with each passing hour,
Where labor's fruits are mine to devour.

Oh, fat mouse, oh, fat mouse,
Don't steal my young crops and arouse.
For years, I've cared for you, I espouse.
Night and day, who consoles my vows?
I swear to leave you, for that's the plan,
To a land of peace, far from the fat man.
A land where we eat what we earn, understand,
And we sigh no more, hand in hand.

TANG POETRY (唐风)

"Tang Feng" refers to the music of the Tang region. King Cheng of Zhou enfeoffed his brother Ji Shuyu in the Tang region, with the capital city located in what is now the southern part of Yicheng County, Shanxi Province. The Tang region was situated near the Jin River and later changed its state name to Jin. The land was barren, and the people were poor, but they were diligent, frugal, and possessed deep thoughts. The poetry from this region reflects their hardships in life and their dissatisfaction with rulers. There are twelve surviving poems in the Tang Feng collection, all believed to be works from the Eastern Zhou period. The style of these poems is somewhat similar to the "Wei Feng," and they often express melancholic and bitter sentiments, reflecting the sorrows of life.

THE CRICKET (蟋蟀)

In the cold weather, crickets enter the hall,
A year passes by in haste, winter will befall.
If we don't enjoy life when we may,
The fleeting days and months will not stay.
Balancing pleasure and responsibility we must strive,
Don't neglect your duties in this life.
Maintain your integrity, yet take time to thrive,
Wise men are those who heed this advice.

In the cold weather, crickets enter the hall,
A year passes by in haste, and we may fall.
If we don't enjoy life when we may,
The fleeting days and months don't delay.
Balancing pleasure and responsibility is key,
Handling extra affairs successfully.
Maintain your integrity, and joyful you'll be,
Wise men know how to handle life gracefully.

In the cold weather, crickets enter the hall,
Ceasing from work, the vehicles rest, and all.
If we don't enjoy life when we may,
The fleeting days and months slip away.
Balancing pleasure and responsibility, stay aware,
For national affairs, we all should care.
Maintain your integrity, in leisure, be aware,
Wise men know how to live without despair.

MOUNTAIN SUMAC (山有枢)

On the mountain stands a tree called sumac so high,
In the lowland grows a tree named elm nearby.
You have clothes and garments, there's no need to buy,
Unused, they sit, in your chest, oh my oh my.
You have horses and carriages, there's no deny,
Unridden, they stay, never on the fly.
One day, when you close your eye,
Others will enjoy, and sigh.

On the mountain stands a tree, the koa tree tall,
In the lowland grows a tree, the tallow tree in thrall.
You have a yard and houses, don't let them fall,
Neglected, they become dirty, oh that's not small.
You have bells and drums in your hall,
Unsounded, they are, silent, not a call.
One day, when you close your eyes in the hall,
Others will occupy your home and all.

On the mountain stands a tree, the lacquer tree's light,
In the lowland grows a tree, the chestnut tree bright.
You have vegetables and wine to enjoy right,
Why not feast and drink, and make the night?
Let's revel and be merry, oh, it's just right,
Let's enjoy the day and evening, oh so tight.
One day, when you close your eyes so tight,
Someone else will dwell in your house, that's right.

YANG RIVER (扬之水)

The small river's waters gently meander and flow,
Underneath, white stones in the water's glow.
Wearing my plain red-embroidered clothes,
I follow you to the road of Quwo.
Having met my lover, my heart aglow,
How can I not be joyful and show?

The small river's waters gently meander and flow,
Underneath, white stones in a crystal row.
Wearing my plain red-embroidered attire so,
I follow you to the riverside below.
Having met my lover, my heart in tow,
Why harbor any sorrow, I wish to know?

The small river's waters gently meander and flow,
Underneath, white stones glitter and throw.
Hearing the news of our secret rendezvous,
I dare not share it with others, I choose.

JIAO LIAO (椒聊)

Peppercorns cluster and hang from the tree,
Heaping, peppercorns ascend merrily.
Look at the woman's son, standing tall,
In stature, he's unmatched, over all.
Like clusters of peppercorns, fragrance free,
Its aroma wafting to a distant spree!

Peppercorns cluster and hang from the tree,
Heaping, peppercorns hold their fragrance spree.
Look at the woman's son, hearty and strong,
With a heart that's loyal all along.
Like clusters of peppercorns, fragrance free,
Its aroma wafting to a distant spree!

CHOU MIAO (绸缪)

Bundles of firewood, tied tight in a twine,
Three stars aloft in the sky do shine.
Tonight, what kind of night could it be?
To meet such a wonderful person, you see.
You, oh you!
What should I do with you?

Bundles of grass, tightly they entwine,
Three stars now in the east do shine.
Tonight, what kind of night could it be?
To meet with the one who's so dear to me.
You, oh you!
How should I handle you?

Bundles of brambles, tied tightly in line,
Three stars' radiant light do brightly shine.
Tonight, what kind of night could it be?
To meet with someone so beautiful to see.
You, oh you!
What should I do with thee?

DI DU (杕杜)

That solitary pear tree stands so high,
Its leaves are lush, reaching for the sky.
I walk alone, feeling rather bleak,
Is there no one who'll walk along this creek?
Not even my kin to share this road's strife,
It's a pity, those people in my life.
Why do they keep such a distance rife?
For help in times of trouble, where's the wife?

That solitary pear tree stands so high,
Its leaves are green, reaching for the sky.
I walk alone, feeling quite forlorn,
Is there no one to whom I can be sworn?
Not even my kinsmen, close and warm,
It's a pity, those people in this form.
Why do they keep themselves in such dorm?
To help a friend in need, where's the norm?

GAO QIU (羔裘)

You wear a leopard-skin sleeved fur robe,
Arrogance in your demeanor you strobe.
Is there no one else in the world, do you see,
Only because you've been so good to me?

You wear a leopard-skin trimmed fur robe,
With arrogance, your attitude, you probe.
Is there no one else in the world, it's true,
Only because you've been so kind and true?

BAO YU (鸨羽)

Wild geese flap their wings with a rustling sound,
Alighting in thickets where zelkova trees are found.
The king's tasks never seem to be complete,
Leaving no time to sow sorghum and wheat.
What will parents rely on to stay fed?
Beneath the vast heavens, I'm filled with dread,
When will there be a place to lay my head?

Wild geese flap their wings with a rustling sound,
Alighting in thickets where thorn bushes abound.
The king's tasks never seem to be done right,
No time to grow millet and rice day and night.
What will parents rely on, the unknown spread?
Beneath the vast heavens, I'm filled with plight,
How long will this period of service take flight?

Wild geese flap their wings with a rustling sound,
Alighting in thickets where mulberry trees are found.
The king's tasks never seem to be complete,
Leaving no time to sow rice and wheat.
What will parents rely on for daily bread?
Beneath the vast heavens, I'm filled with dread,
When will my life return to normal ahead?

WU YI (无衣)

Do I not have clothes to wear, you ask?
I have six or seven garments in my task.
Just not as fine as the clothes you gave,
Yours are comfortable and nicely pave.

Do I not have clothes to wear, you ask?
I have six or seven garments in my task.
Just not as warm as the clothes you gave,
Yours are cozy and comfortable enclave.

YOU DE'S DU (有杕之杜)

There's a solitary pear tree you will find,
Standing tall by the roadside's design.
Oh wise and noble gentleman, I implore,
Will you come closer to me, I implore?
In my heart, I truly adore,
Why not share joy in wine galore?

There's a solitary pear tree by the way,
Standing tall, the right path does convey.
Oh wise and noble gentleman, I implore,
Will you come and frolic with me, I implore?
In my heart, I truly adore,
Why not share joy in wine galore?

GE SHENG (葛生)

Vines of kudzu cover the thorny tree,
Creeping grass spreads, wild and free.
The one I love has left my side,
Who will keep him company, provide?
Alone, in the wilderness, I lie.

Vines of kudzu cover the thorn's embrace,
Creeping grass extends near the resting place.
The one I love has left my side,
Who will keep him company, provide?
Alone, in the wilderness, I sigh.

A splendid canopy and ornate bed,
Golden blankets draped over, it's said.
The one I love has left my side,
Who will keep him company, provide?
Alone, until morning's light, I tread.

Summer days are long, nights are deep,
After a hundred years, we will finally meet.

Nights in winter are long and cold,
After a hundred years, I will return to your fold.

CAI LING (采苓)

Harvesting sweet herbs, oh, harvesting sweet herbs,
On the mountaintop at sunrise, it perturbs.
There are some who love to tell false tales,
Don't pay them heed, let their words set sail.
Don't believe, don't believe what they say,
Their words are untrue, causing dismay.
There are some who love to tell false tales,
Their words will harm, as they trail.

Harvesting bitter herbs, oh, harvesting bitter herbs,
Below First Yang Mountain, their words disturb.
There are some who weave lies from thin air,
Don't befriend them, it's only despair.
Don't believe, don't believe what they say,
Their words are unreliable, keep them at bay.
There are some who weave lies from thin air,
Their false words lead to nowhere.

Harvesting shepherd's purse, oh, harvesting shepherd's
purse,
On the eastern slope, their claims intersperse.
There are some who speak lies with glee,
Don't follow them, it's easy to see.
Don't believe, don't believe what they say,
Their words are not trustworthy, don't sway.
There are some who speak lies with glee,
They gain nothing in the end, you'll agree.

QIN FENG (秦风)

Qin was originally a vassal state of the Zhou dynasty. During the reign of King Xuan of Zhou, Qin Zhong was sent to suppress the Western Rong but failed and was killed. When King Ping of Zhou moved to the east, Duke Xiang, the grandson of Qin Zhong, escorted him and was granted the title of a vassal state. Qin thus officially became a vassal state. At this time, it had an area of eight hundred li (ancient Chinese unit of distance), and later Duke De moved to Yong, which is now Fengxiang County in Shaanxi. The area controlled by Qin roughly corresponds to the central part of modern Shaanxi and the southeastern part of Gansu. The "Qin Feng" poems are from this region and consist of ten poems, mainly about chariots, horses, fields, and hunting, reflecting a martial spirit. However, there are poems like "Jian Jia" that are graceful and beautiful.

CHE LIN (车邻)

Chariots run, wheels clattering loud,
The charioteer holds reins, riding proud.
For a long time, I haven't seen you here,
Just waiting for the monk to make it clear.

Lacquer trees grow on the hillside's face,
In low-lying areas, chestnuts find their place.
Now that I've seen your noble grace,
Let's sit together, playing harp and bass.
Now, enjoyment delayed, what's the case?
In the blink of an eye, old age we embrace.

Mulberry trees grow on the mountainside,
In low-lying areas, willows provide.
Now that I've seen your noble grace,
Let's sit together, playing flute and side.
Now, enjoyment delayed, it's a ride,
Time passes swiftly, joy can't reside.

SI LING (駟驖)

Four black steeds, strong and bold,
The charioteer's hand grasps reins of gold.
The noble son Qin loves most of all,
Goes to the hunting grounds at his call.

Palace officials drive out full-grown game,
Fat and sturdy, they're everywhere the same.
Qin's lord commands, chase to the left,
Arrows fly, hunting scenes deft.

Hunting done, to the northern park they steer,
Four steeds' steps gentle, without fear.
Light chariots, phoenix bells chime clear,
Hunting hounds rest, gathered near.

XIAO RONG (小戎)

The war chariot is light, the carriage shallow,
Five leather straps twist around the yoke's hallow.
Around the waist, a belt for urging the steed,
Pulling the cart, leather reins proceed.
Cushion adorned with patterns, carriage hub long,
Driving a flowered horse, the whip goes strong.
Thinking of my husband with character so strong,
He's as gentle as jade, where I belong.

Four strong horses, fit and well,
The driver holds six reins as he sets the spell.
Green horses and red horses in the center line,
Yellow horses and black horses behind, they shine.
Dragon-patterned shields together combine,
Copper rings of bridles, a linked design.
Thinking of my husband with character so fine,
When he's at home, warmth does entwine.

Four horses, light and nimble, in harmony stride,
Spears with three-sided shafts, in copper they bide.
Large shields with beautiful patterns to guide,
Leopard-skin bow covers, gold carving beside.
Two bows intersect, quiver fastened with pride,
Bowstring coils, in the pouch do confide.
Thinking of my husband with traits so wide,
Sometimes awake, sometimes in dreams, abide.

JIAN JIA (蒹葭)

By the river, green reeds stretch so wide,
In deep autumn, white dew turns to frost outside.
The one I yearn for, oh, where does he reside?
Just on the other side of the water's tide.
Against the current, I search far and wide,
The path is perilous, on this endless ride.
With the current, along the bank, I stride,
As if he's in the middle of the water, my guide.

By the river, reeds dense and high,
As the sun rises, dew glistens in the sky.
The one I yearn for, oh, where does he lie?
Just on the other side, I can't deny.
Against the current, a treacherous path to try,
The road is rough, making me sigh.
With the current, along the bank, I apply,
As if he's on an island nearby.

By the river, reeds dense and thick,
Early morning dew, still making them slick.
The one I yearn for, just on the opposite side,
Against the current, the path is hard to pick.
With the current, along the bank, I stick,
As if he's on an island across the creek.

ZHONG NAN (终南)

What do you find atop Mount Zhongnan?
Lush mountain oaks and plum trees, they plan.
Today, a nobleman arrives with grace,
Wearing splendid attire, a fox fur embrace.
His face is rosy like painted in a vase,
Is this our ruler, we must now embrace?

What do you find atop Mount Zhongnan?
Valuable Chinese cherries and sweet osmanthus span.
Today, a nobleman arrives at this site,
Adorned in colorful garments, a wondrous sight.
Jade tinkles on him, sparkling in the light,
The emperor's grace, forever in our might.

HUANG NIAO (黄鸟)

Little yellow bird chirps so gay,
Lands on a jujube tree on display.
Who accompanies Duke Mu in his grave,
Zi Che, departed, that's his name.
Speaking of this departed dame,
None could match his virtue or fame.
People approach his tomb in shame,
Shivering, grieving, their hearts aflame.
Infinite heavens high above our frame,
Unjustly, good men are slain.
If we could redeem his life's claim,
With a hundred men, we'd play the game.

Little yellow bird chirps so clear,
Lands on a mulberry tree, spreading cheer.
Who accompanies Duke Mu in his rest,
Zi Che Zhongxing, by many, esteemed best.
Speaking of this esteemed guest,
His virtues outshine all the rest.
People approach his tomb, feeling pressed,
Shivering, grieving, by pain obsessed.
Infinite heavens, justice manifest,
Unjustly, good men are oppressed.
If we could redeem his life's quest,
With a hundred men, we'd stand the test.

Little yellow bird chirps in the breeze,
Lands on a thorny tree with ease.
Who accompanies Duke Mu in the tomb,
Zi Che Zhen Hu, dispelling gloom.
Speaking of this exceptional groom,
His virtues outshine others' bloom.
People approach his tomb in the gloom,

Shivering, grieving, their hearts consume.
Infinite heavens, justice will resume,
Unjustly, good men face their doom.
If we could redeem his life's resume,
With a hundred men, we'd dispel the gloom.

MORNING BREEZE (晨风)

The morning breeze, birds swiftly soar,
They return to the lush trees in the north once more.
It's been so long since I've seen my husband's face,
Anxious and worried, thoughts in every place.
What can I do? What can I say?
Has he, perhaps, forgotten me today?

Clusters of oak trees cover the hillside wide,
Red plum trees grow by the riverside.
It's been so long since I've seen my husband's face,
Anxious and melancholy, day by day's embrace.
What can I do? What can I say?
Has he, perhaps, forgotten me today?

Clusters of catalpa trees adorn the hill's expanse,
Thick Chinese yew trees in the wetland dance.
It's been so long since I've seen my husband's face,
As if drunk, my spirit has left its place.
What can I do? What can I say?
Has he, perhaps, forgotten me today?

NO CLOTHES (无衣)

Who said we had no clothing to wear?
We don battle robes, side by side, our share.
The king raises an army, it's time to prepare,
Quickly mend the spears and swords we bear.
Together, we'll seek vengeance, fair and square.

Who said we had no clothing to wear?
We don linen shirts, a matching pair.
The king raises an army, it's time to beware,
Hastily mend the halberds, ready to declare,
Side by side, we'll face the enemy, without a tear.

Who said we had no clothing to wear?
We don battle tunics, a matching affair.
The king raises an army, we must be aware,
Swiftly mend the armor and sharpen each glaive,
Together, we march to battle, brave and unswayed.

WEI YANG (渭阳)

I sent my uncle,
Sent him to Wei Yang.
What gift shall I give to him?
A carriage and four horses for his yang.

I sent my uncle,
My thoughts are long.
What gift shall I give to him?
Beautiful jade ornaments to adorn him strong.

QUAN YU (权舆)

Oh, me!
Once I lived in tall towers, so grand,
Now every meal is eaten out of hand.
Oh, dear, dear!
I can't relive those days so grand.

Oh, me!
Once four dishes graced my table fine,
Now every meal, I can't seem to dine.
Oh, dear, dear!
I can't relive those moments, so fine.

CHEN FENG (陈风)

"Chen Feng" refers to the music style from the Chen region. Chen was located in the area that is now Huaiyang, Zhecheng, and Bozhou in Henan and Anhui provinces. After King Wu conquered the Shang dynasty, he appointed Gui Man, a descendant of Emperor Shun, as the ruler of Chen and married his eldest daughter to Gui Man. Chen was situated in the southern part of the Zhou kingdom, neighboring the Wu and Chu regions. The land was flat, with no notable mountains or rivers. The people of Chen were gentle in nature, believed in spirits and ghosts, and had less of the northern resoluteness and more of the southern charm. There are ten poems that remain from this region, most of which describe marriage customs and songs and dances.

YUAN QIU (宛丘)

Your dance moves, swirling and spinning,
Dancing atop Yuan Qiu's haven.
I truly admire you, my heart is yearning,
But alas, there's no hope in returning.

The drums resound with a cheerful ring,
Dancing on Yuan Qiu, a beautiful thing.
Regardless of winter or the heat of spring,
White egret feathers you artfully fling.

The drums strike, their rhythm singing,
Dancing on Yuan Qiu's pathway, a stunning wing.
Regardless of winter or the heat of spring,
Egret feathers adorn you, a royal bling.

EAST GATE SCENES (东门之景)

Outside the East Gate, the white elms stand tall,
On Wanqiu Hill, rows of oak trees enthrall.
The good girl from the Zizhong family,
Under the trees, dances gracefully and free.

Choosing a good day, we head south to the highlands,
No more busy weaving hemp threads in our hands.
In the bustling city, we'll dance and play,
On this beautiful day, together we'll sway.

We set off on this wonderful day,
A crowd gathers, forming a line in a display.
You, like the morning glory, enchanting and bright,
Gift me a handful of fragrant Sichuan pepper spice.

HENG GATE (衡门)

A simple door made of crossbeams and wood,
A place to rest and shelter, it's understood.
Clear water flows gently and long,
Sating hunger with its pure song.

Must we eat fish to satisfy our craving,
Only Yellow River carp for a feast worth saving?
Must we take a wife, is that the way,
Only a maiden from the state of Qi may stay?

Must we eat fish to relish the delight,
Only Yellow River carp to make it right?
Must we take a wife, is that the key,
Only a maiden from the state of Song shall it be?

EAST GATE POND (东门之池)

Outside the East Gate, a protective city moat,
Used as a place for soaking and to gloat.
A beautiful and kind young lady so fine,
We can sing together, her beauty divine.

Outside the East Gate, a protective trench it seems,
Used as a spot for soaking and to dream.
A beautiful and kind young lady so fair,
We can chat about life, our hearts laid bare.

Outside the East Gate, a protective moat so clear,
Used as a place for soaking, no need to fear.
A beautiful and kind young lady so sweet,
We can share our feelings, our hearts shall meet.

EAST GATE POPLARS (东门之杨)

Outside the East Gate, there are white poplar trees,
Branches lush, a place that surely pleases.
We agree to meet at twilight's gentle grace,
Waiting for the stars to brightly embrace.

Outside the East Gate, the white poplars sway,
In the wind, their leaves rustle and play.
We agree to meet at twilight's tender light,
Waiting for the morning star to shine so bright.

GRAVEYARD GATE (墓门)

At the graveyard gate, a sour jujube tree stands tall,
I pick up an axe and give it a heavy fall.
That man, not of virtuous kin,
The whole country knows of his sin.
He knows, yet he won't amend,
His past actions, he won't defend.

At the graveyard gate, a sour jujube tree, an owl's domain,
That man, not virtuous, it's plain.
I sing, advising him to see the light,
To mend his ways before it's too late, it's right.

GUARDING A MAGPIE'S NEST (防有鹊巢)

Have you ever seen a dyke built high for a magpie's nest?
Have you ever seen a hill with long grass, a peaceful rest?
Who's sowing discord in my love's sweet nest?
My heart is troubled, it can't be put to rest.

Have you ever seen a courtyard with tiles that gleam?
Have you ever seen a mountain with silk grass it does seem?
Who's sowing discord in my love's sweet nest?
My heart is fearful, causing me distress.

MOONRISE (月出)

The bright moon rises high in the sky,
A beautiful lady with a graceful sigh.
She walks slowly with a charming grace,
Thinking of her sets my heart's pace.

The clear moon shines in the sky so high,
A beauty beneath, catches my eye.
Her gentle steps, a charming embrace,
Thinking of her fills my heart's space.

The brilliant moon in the night's domain,
A beauty beneath, her allure I can't restrain.
Her graceful walk, a captivating trace,
Thinking of her fills my heart with base.

ZHULIN (株林)

Why do we go to Zhulin, you ask?
Not for a leisurely stroll, it's quite a task.
It's not about visiting Zhulin for fun,
But to find Xia Nan, the only one.

I drive my horse-drawn carriage with haste,
Outside Zhulin, I dismount in haste.
Switch to my agile horse so fast,
To Zhulin, we ride for breakfast at last.

ZE BI (泽陂)

Around the pond, embankments rise so high,
With reeds and lotus, a pleasing sigh.
Over there is a beauty so fair,
I love her, and it's beyond compare.
Day and night, thoughts of her occupy,
Tears flow, a constant, sorrowful cry.

Around the pond, the embankment stands tall,
With lotus and reeds, a charming sprawl.
Over there is a beauty so fine,
Her grace and charm, forever mine.
Day and night, thoughts of her appall,
Restless, my heart's in turmoil, a bitter thrall.

Around the pond, embankments reach the sky,
With lotus and reeds, a captivating nigh.
Over there is a beauty, oh, so dear,
Her elegance and poise, I hold near.
Day and night, thoughts of her belie,
Anxious, my heart's burdened, tears dry.

KUAI FENG (桧风)

The "Kuai Wind" is a melody from the region of Huidi, which encompasses present-day Zhengzhou, Xinzhen, Xingyang, and Mi County in Henan, China. Its ruler was of the Yun clan, a descendant of Zhurong. During the early reign of King Ping of Zhou, it was annexed by Duke Wu of Zheng and became part of the Zheng state. Four poems from this region have survived, and they are generally considered to have been composed before the downfall of Kuai, displaying a melancholic and somber tone.

LAMB'S FUR ROBE (羔裘)

When you roam leisurely in your lamb's fur robe,
And wear your fox-fur cape when you head to the court,
How can I not be filled with sorrow and woe?
Anxious and restless, my heart is distraught.

When you stroll around, wearing a lamb's fur attire,
And don your fox-fur cape when your duties require,
How can I not be filled with sorrow and care?
Thinking of you, my heart is burdened, I swear.

In your lamb's fur robe, so pristine and fair,
In the sunlight, it gleams with a radiant air.
How can I not be filled with sorrow and woe?
The sadness within me, how can it go?

WHITE CAP (素冠)

Seeing you in a white cap's attire,
Your thin figure, it does inspire,
My heart is overwhelmed with sorrow's fire.

Seeing you in a white garment's grace,
My heart sinks into a sorrowful place,
With you, I long to share a living space.

Seeing you in a white skirt's embrace,
Sorrow within me starts to efface,
With you, I want to face life's chase.

SAWTOOTH OAK AND HARDY REED
(隰有萇楚)

In the lowlands, sheep's peaches grow,
Vines entwine, their branches in tow.
Fresh and lush, they thrive and show,
I envy their carefree life, you know.

In the lowlands, sheep's peaches spread,
Vines entwine, flowers grace their bed.
Fresh and lush, their growth widespread,
I envy their worry-free lives instead.

In the lowlands, sheep's peaches abound,
Fruit-laden vines hang all around.
Fresh and lush, their growth unbound,
I envy their lack of home and sound.

NOT THE WIND (匪风)

The wind howls, a relentless sound,
The chariot races, the pace unbound.
Looking back at the path I'm bound,
Longing for home, my heart is profound.

The wind howls, spinning around,
The chariot races, dangers abound.
Looking back at the path I'm bound,
Longing for home, tears gather and mound.

Who will cook the fish and make the meal,
I'll wash the dishes, it's a fair deal.
Who will return to the west, I appeal,
To bring news and ensure we're still real.

CAO FENG (曹风)

The land of Cao was situated in present-day Shandong, including Heze, Dingtao, and Caozhou. King Wu of Zhou enfeoffed his brother, Shu Zhenduo, in this region, but it was later conquered by the state of Song during the 5th century BCE. Four poems from this area have survived, reflecting themes of life's fleeting nature, the vicissitudes of fortune, satire of petty individuals, and praise for Lord Xun. These poems were recorded to document the customs of the region, though the state was small and the poems are considered of minor importance.

MAYFLY (蜉蝣)

Mayfly with your fluttering wings,
In bright garments, a beauty that sings.
How can I not be filled with sorrow's sting?
Where is my homecoming, my everything?

Mayfly, as you soar in the air,
In resplendent attire, beyond compare.
How can I not be filled with sorrow's care?
My thoughts of home, so heavy to bear.

Mayfly, emerging from earth to reside,
In linen robes, white as snow's guide.
How can I not be filled with sorrow's tide?
Where will I find my final stride?

WARDEN (候人)

The low-ranking warden, simple and plain,
Carries a long spear and a staff with disdain.
In the court, there are nobles, a newfangled train,
Three hundred attendants, in robes that remain.

The heron perches above the fish dam's lair,
Its wings stay dry, the water it doesn't share.
In the court, there are nobles, a newfangled glare,
How can these pretenders, in noble attire, compare?

The heron perches above the fish dam's flow,
Its beak stays dry, as it should, we all know.
In the court, there are nobles, a newfangled show,
Favored for a while, but their fortunes may go.

The clouds are vast, and the mist does roll,
In the southern mountains, a morning rainbow unfolds.
A delicate maiden, with her heart and soul,
Hungry and alone, without a bowl.

THE TURTLEDOVES (鸤鸠)

The turtledoves build nests on the mulberry tree,
Raising many little birds with glee.
The virtuous and noble gentlemen,
Their appearance remains consistently beautiful then.
Their appearance remains consistently beautiful then,
With steadfast hearts and principles, again and again.

The turtledoves build nests on the mulberry tree,
Little birds play amidst the plum's decree.
The virtuous and noble gentlemen,
Around their waists, a broad sash is seen.
Around their waists, a black leather hat's esteem,
In elegant attire, they gleam and sheen.

The turtledoves build nests on the mulberry tree,
Little birds chirp amidst the jujube's spree.
The virtuous and noble gentlemen,
Their appearance unchanged, like a refrain.
Their appearance unchanged, as a standard they
maintain,
Nations learn from them, their ways to sustain.

The turtledoves build nests on the mulberry tree,
Little birds frolic among the hazelnut's glee.
The virtuous and noble gentlemen,
Beloved by the people, their trust and devotion keen.
Beloved by the people, may they reign supreme,
Wishing them a long life, an eternal dream.

BENEATH THE SPRING (下泉)

Cold spring water bubbles forth,
Soaking the clumps of dogtail grass henceforth.
Upon waking, I cannot help but sigh,
Remembering the prosperous Zhou dynasty, oh my.

Cold spring water bubbles forth in might,
Soaking the clumps of wormwood in sight.
Upon waking, I cannot help but sigh,
The royal capital, haunting dreams apply.

Cold spring water bubbles forth with grace,
Soaking the clumps of wild mugwort's embrace.
Upon waking, I cannot help but sigh,
Yearning for the capital where sleep does not belie.

The millet seedlings grow tall and strong,
Watered by rain, it won't be long.
Lords from various states come along,
To confer with Count Huan, in honor, they throng.

BIN FENG (豳风)

The "BIN Feng" is a musical melody from the region of Bin, which corresponds to the modern area of Bin County and Xunyi in Shaanxi Province. It was originally the territory of the forefather of the Zhou dynasty, Duke Liu Kai. When King Ping of Zhou moved eastward, Bin became part of the state of Qin. It is believed that the "BIN Feng" was composed during the early Western Zhou period, making it one of the oldest poems in the "Guofeng" section of the Book of Songs. These poems often focus on agricultural and rural themes, reflecting the importance of farming and the roots of Chinese culture. There are seven poems in this section, with "The Seventh Month" being a typical agricultural poem. Several poems also have strong connections to the eastern region, such as "The Axe" and "Eastern Mountain." There is a traditional belief that these poems are associated with the Duke of Zhou, who played a significant role in the Zhou dynasty's rule and is also connected to the state of Lu in the east. This has led some to refer to the "BIN Feng" as the "Lu Songs," as it is thought that they may have been collected by Western Zhou people during their expeditions to the east and performed using the melodies of the Bin region.

SEVENTH MONTH (七月)

In the seventh month, Mars veers to the west,
In the ninth month, people sew their clothes.
In November, the northern wind howls,
In December, bone-chilling cold abounds.
With coarse clothes and short jackets,
How shall we endure the winter?
In January, we repair our farming tools,
In February, we rush to cultivate the fields.
Wives and children accompany us,
Bringing meals to the fields.
The local officials visit, delighted.

In the seventh month, Mars veers to the west,
In the ninth month, people sew their clothes.
The sun of spring is warmly shining,
And the orioles sing from the branches.
Girls carry deep bamboo baskets,
Gathering diligently along the small path,
Collecting tender mulberry leaves.
The daylight in spring is indeed long,
Baskets of artemisia are gathered.
The maiden picking artemisia is filled with sorrow,
Fearing that a young man will take her away.

In the seventh month, Mars veers to the west,
In August, people harvest reeds and cut rushes.
During the silkworm season, we trim the mulberry trees,
Lifting our axes with raised arms.
Trimming the long branches and twigs to make them clean,
Pulling short branches to gather tender mulberry leaves.
In July, the orioles sing merrily,
In August, we spin hemp and weave fabric busily.

Dyeing it in black or yellow,
I dye it red, vibrant and bright,
To make clothes for that young man.

In April, the Artemisia argyi bears seeds,
In May, cicadas sing loudly.
In August, crops are harvested tirelessly,
In October, fallen leaves are scattered by the wind.
In November, we're busy hunting dogs and badgers,
And we have to skin foxes,
To make winter clothing for that young man.
In December, everyone gathers for a feast,
Continuing hunting and training diligently.
Little pigs are eaten by us,
While big ones are sent to the authorities.

In May, grasshoppers leap and chirp,
In June, weaving girls flutter their wings and sing.
In July, crickets sing in the wild,
In August, they sing under the eaves.
In September, they enter the house,
In October, they hide beneath the bed.
Fumigating to drive away mice,
Sealing the straw doors and closing the north windows.
After finishing work, we call our wives and children,
Seeing the new year approaching,
We'll live in this room.

In June, we eat plums and grapes,
In July, we cook kohlrabi and soybeans.
In August, we beat the jujubes from the tree,
In October, we thresh the rice in the field.
Fermented into spring wine, fragrant to the nose,
Praying for longevity and well-being.
In July, we eat sweet melons like honey,
In August, we harvest bottle gourds from the vines,
In September, sesame seeds are stored.

Prepare wild vegetables and firewood,
Farmers rely on this to pass the time.

In September, the threshing grounds are prepared,
In October, the grains go into the granary.
Millet, sorghum, and highland barley,
Along with millet, beans, and wheat.
I lament the hardships of a farmer's life,
Working in the fields has just been completed,
Now we must labor for the authorities.
In the daytime, we cut thatch in the wilderness,
At night, we twist ropes until dawn.
Hastily repairing the house,
The sowing season has come again.

In December, we chip ice, making a resounding noise,
In January, we deliver it to the ice cellar.
In February, we hold ancestor-worship ceremonies,
Offering leeks and lambs.
In September, the sky is high, the air crisp,
In October, we clean the threshing grounds.
Presenting two bottles of sweet rice wine,
Slaughtering big and small lambs.
Climbing the steps into the hall,
Lifting up cow-horn cups,
In unison, we offer wishes for "endless longevity."

SCREECH OWL (鸱鸮)

Screech owl, oh, screech owl, I plea,
You've taken my fledglings, can't you see?
Don't destroy my nest with glee,
I've toiled and worried endlessly.

While the weather's fair and not a drop,
Quickly peel some mulberry bark atop,
Fix the doors and windows, make them stop.
Now, whoever dares to intrude or flop,
Underneath our roof, let them be mop.

I'm worn and my hands are stiff,
Gathering wild herbs for nest relief.
I've stored provisions for winter's grief,
But my beak is sore, beyond belief,
Our nest's security, in disbelief.

My feathers resemble withered grass,
My tail's scarce, a fleeting pass.
Our nest, precarious, it may amass,
Rocked by storms, in every class,
Scaring us, a shrill sound, alas.

EASTERN MOUNTAIN (东山)

I went to Eastern Mountain for a battle,
Long unable to return to my hometown's prattle.
Today, I return from the East once more,
In a drizzle of fine rain, my body I implore.

I just heard I'm going home, it's true,
Gazing westward, my heart feels blue.
Dressed in commoner's clothes anew,
No more war with spears, I construe.
Silkworms crawl slowly, steadily they're due,
In the wild, mulberry trees, their venue.
I curl my body, a tight ball to construe,
Sleeping beneath the war chariot, it's true.

I went to Eastern Mountain for a battle,
Long unable to return to my hometown's prattle.
Today, I return from the East once more,
In a drizzle of fine rain, my body I implore.
Small melons and gourds in clusters they score,
Vines hanging long, from the roof they explore.
Inside, the house damp, turtles on the floor,
Doors and windows cloaked in cobweb galore.
Fields become deer's domain, they soar,
At night, fireflies illuminate, never a bore.
Homestead deserted, but not a sore,
Still, in my heart, a cherished rapport.

I went to Eastern Mountain for a battle,
Long unable to return to my hometown's prattle.
Today, I return from the East once more,
In a drizzle of fine rain, my body I implore.
Storks stand atop earth mounds, deplore,
Wife at home, sighing forevermore.

Sweeping the house, repairs galore,
Awaiting my return, they implore.
Bitter gourds hang, bitter for sure,
On chestnut wood and piled ashore.
Since we parted, tears we deplore,
Three years now, day and night, I explore.

I went to Eastern Mountain for a battle,
Long unable to return to my hometown's prattle.
Today, I return from the East once more,
In a drizzle of fine rain, my body I implore.
Warblers flutter, in the sky they outpour,
Feathers glistening, shining evermore.
Thinking of her as a bride she wore,
A red and yellow dress, a memory we adore.
Her mother tied a jade pendant to implore,
Various rituals for good fortune they explore.
Beautiful spring wedding, days of yore,
Now, our reunion, what will it restore?

THE AXE (破斧)

The battle-axe is already damaged and worn,
The great adze too, its defects borne.
Duke Zhou's expedition to the East is sworn,
Four states shudder at his return.
Duke Zhou pities our common folk's concern,
His boundless virtue we shall discern.

The battle-axe is already damaged and worn,
The battle-hoe too, with blemishes torn.
Duke Zhou's expedition to the East is known,
Four states now feel his influence grown.
Duke Zhou pities our common folk's concern,
His virtuous deeds, a tale to be shown.

The battle-axe is shattered, signs of strife,
The battle-shovel too, with cracks rife.
Duke Zhou's expedition brings peace to life,
The four states find tranquility rife.
Duke Zhou pities our common folk's strife,
His virtue's renown, spreading far and wide.

FELLING OAK TREES (伐柯)

How to make an axe handle?
Without an axe head, it's incomplete.
How to marry a wife?
Without a matchmaker, it won't proceed.

To make an axe handle, oh, to make an axe handle,
The guidelines are not far from you.
I've met a lovely maiden,
The dishes she sets out are truly beautiful.

NINE SONGS (九罭)

A fine-meshed net captures a big salmon trout,
I behold this esteemed guest, without a doubt.
Dressed in dragon-patterned, splendid attire,
Geese along the waterside soar higher and higher.

The master returns, no place to stay the night,
Stay here for two evenings, it seems just right.
The geese fly high above the land's might,
Stay two more nights, is that alright?

So he hides his embroidered dragon robes from view,
Don't let my master leave, it's what I implore,
Don't make my heart troubled and sore.

WOLF RUNNING (狼跋)

The old wolf moves forward, stepping on its jaw,
Then it retreats, crushing its long tail, not a flaw.
Gongsun's form is graceful, with a step so sure,
Feet clad in red shoes, he treads the floor.

The old wolf moves backward, stepping on its tail,
Then it advances, crushing its fat chin without fail.
Gongsun's form is graceful, his reputation pure,
His virtues and fame, forever endure.

YA (雅)

"Ya" is a type of music that originated in the vicinity of the royal capital during the Zhou Dynasty. According to Zhu Xi's "Collected Works of Poetry," he said, "Ya is the proper music, the song of correct music. In its pieces, there is a distinction between small and large, and Confucian scholars each have their own interpretations of correctness and variations. Based on current understanding, Small Ya is the music for feasting and entertainment, while Large Ya is the music for court meetings and delivering admonitions."

According to Zhu's interpretation, "Ya" can be categorized as small or large, likely related to the scale of the performance and the official or folk context in which it was performed. Small Ya was played during feasts and entertainment, while Large Ya was performed during court meetings. However, Huizhou Ti's "Poetry Commentary" believes that "small and large Ya" should be distinguished by the music itself, not by the significance of the political context, just as there are both small and large modes in the Lv music.

XIAO YA (小雅)

"Xiao Ya" consists of seventy-four poems, most of which were created during the late Western Zhou period and the early Eastern Zhou period. The authors included upper-class nobles as well as commoners. The content of the poems is extensive and rich, depicting various aspects of the social life of the time. It exposes and criticizes the corruption and darkness in the political landscape of the era. Additionally, it includes works related to agriculture, sacrifices, banquets, gifts, and expressions of feelings relevant to the time.

DEER CRY (鹿鸣)

The deer call out ceaselessly, not ceasing its plea,
Summoning companions to dine with glee.
I have esteemed guests filling the hall so free,
For them, I play the se and blow the sheng, as you see.

I play the sheng and blow the heng in glee,
Presenting gifts in abundance, for all to see.
All the guests appreciate my company,
Explaining principles and pointing the way, agree.

The deer call out ceaselessly, not ceasing its plea,
Summoning companions to feast on herbs, you see.
I have esteemed guests filling the hall with glee,
Speaking with elegance and wisdom so spree.
Displaying kindness and generosity with no fee,
These virtuous scholars make an excellent spree.

I have fine wine to offer to my guests, you see,
The esteemed guests drink heartily, joyously free.

THE FOUR HORSES (四牡)

Four horses pull the carriage, rushing on their way,
The road is winding, to a distant place, they sway.
Could it be that I don't miss my home each day?
National affairs are endless, they say.
Causing my heart to be filled with dismay.

Four horses pull the carriage, in haste, they race,
Black-maned white horses, a tired trace.
Could it be that I don't miss my home's embrace?
National affairs are endless, in this case,
No moment for leisure, we face.

Partridges frolic and dance in the air,
Flying up and down, without a care.
Landing on thick oak trees there,
National affairs never cease to prepare,
No respite to feed the father, it's fair.

Ring doves flutter, soar in the air,
Flying and stopping, playfully, beware.
Landing on thick jujube trees with care,
National affairs never cease to declare,
No time to nourish the mother, spare.

Four horses pull the carriage, strong and quick,
Non-stop galloping, the path is thick.
Could it be that I don't miss my family, slick?
I composed this song to make my mother tick,
To remember her, it's quite a trick.

AUSPICIOUS BLESSINGS (吉日)

Flowers bloom in vibrant array,
On plateaus and lowlands, in full display.
Leading my people on this journey's array,
Worried if our mission goes astray.

My horse is strong and full of might,
Six reins are soft, pliable, and tight.
Whip raised high, we ride through day and night,
Seeking wisdom broadly, with all our might.

My horse, robust, with reins so right,
Six strands smooth as silk, a shining light.
Whip raised high, we hasten through our flight,
Extensively inquire, our thoughts ignite.

Snow-white horse with black mane's grace,
Six reins, resilient, in the race.
Whip raised high, we speed up the pace,
Comprehensive inquiries, we embrace.

Horse with black and white, in harmonious line,
Six reins steady, each one in twine.
Whip raised high, we swiftly align,
Careful inquiries, our thoughts refine.

CHANGDI (常棣)

Tang and date flowers, so vividly bright,
Petals and sepals closely unite.
Look at the people in today's light,
None can compare to brothers so right.

In life's cycle, aging and disease cause fright,
Only brothers truly hold you tight.
In a desolate field where tombstones take flight,
Only brothers seek, with all their might.

The lark descends upon a lofty height,
Brothers rush to rescue, with all their might.
Though good friends may stand in sight,
In times of trouble, brothers take flight.

At home, quarrels may ignite,
But against outsiders, we reunite.
Though friends may seem polite,
Over time, their aid may wane in spite.

When chaos subsides, all is set right,
Days of peace and tranquility, a pure delight.
In these moments, with brothers so tight,
Joyful gatherings, hearts light.

Husband and wife in harmonious sight,
Musical instruments in hand, side by side.
Brotherly bonds, feelings ignite,
As the family gathers, spirits unite.

A harmonious family, thriving and bright,
Wife, children, and joy, a true delight.
Careful planning and discussions, all is right,

This is the way, indeed, we should incite.

LOGGING (伐木)

The sound of woodcutting, clang, clang, clang,
Birds singing, their voices rang.
Birds from deep valleys and mountains sang,
Flying to tall trees where they hang.
Birds singing, their pleas, they bang,
Seeking friends and companions, in a pang.
See, it's just a group of birds, a gang,
With their incessant pleas that hang.
How can we, humans, our friendships fang?
To live without friends, that would be a pang.
The deities hear my wishful sang,
And grant us humans harmony and a yang.

The sound of sawing, a loud twang,
New, filtered wine, aromatic and sprang.
Roasting tender lamb, the dinner's bang,
Quickly invite uncles and cousins to clang.
Better he comes for a reason than a wang,
Otherwise, people may find it a yang.
Inside the house, clean and dang,
Eight platters of food on the table rang.
Now that we have tender lamb to yang,
Quickly invite elders; don't let them fang.
Even if he has a reason for his wang,
Don't let others say it's a pang.

Woodcutters arrive on a hill's tang,
Bringing full cups of wine to clang.
Plates and bowls placed, a yang,
Brothers gathered, bonds hang.
Why do some friendships go pang?
Often because of inadequate yang.
If you have wine at home, bring it to yang,

If you don't, go out and buy some tang.
Drums beat, sounding a loud twang,
Dancing joyously, sleeves go yang.
Taking advantage of today's yang,
We enjoy this fine wine, free from a pang.

HEAVENLY BLESSING (天保)

May Heaven bless you with peace,
A firm throne and a prosperous nation.
May your country's strength double,
What kind of blessings and fortune will not be bestowed
upon you?
May your wealth overflow day by day,
There is nothing that won't prosper.

May Heaven bless you with peace,
Enjoying blessings and peace.
All things will be suitable for you,
Receiving countless blessings from Heaven.
May your fortune be long-lasting,
Enjoying it day in and day out.

May Heaven bless you with peace,
There is nothing that won't flourish.
Blessings are like towering mountains,
Stretching like hills and peaks.
Flowing like rivers,
There is nothing that won't increase day by day.

On auspicious days, bathe and offer wine and food,
Respectfully present offerings to ancestors.
In all four seasons, stay busy with rituals,
Offering sacrifices to your ancestors and kings.
Ancestral words pass down, "Wishing you
Endless longevity and thousands of years."

The deities are moved to descend,
Bestowing blessings and good fortune upon you.
Your people are simple and content,
Satisfied with their food and drink.

Common people and officials alike,
Are universally grateful for your kindness.

You are like the ever-present moon in the sky,
You are like the rising sun in the east.
You are like the eternal longevity of the southern
mountains,
Never diminishing, never collapsing.
You are like the flourishing pine and cypress trees,
Both blessings and longevity inherited from you.

GATHERING EDIBLE GREENS (采薇)

Gathering edible greens, oh gathering edible greens,
The edible greens have already sprouted.
Saying "return home," oh, the road back home,
Another year has quickly passed by.
Without a wife, without a family,
Engaged in battle with the Xiongnu.
No leisure, no rest,
I must engage in fierce combat with them.

Gathering edible greens, oh gathering edible greens,
Gathering those tender sprouts of greens.
Saying "return home," oh, the path back home,
Anxiety and thoughts run wild like tangled threads.
Worry and distress burn like fire,
Hungry and thirsty, the days are hard to endure.
Stationed in various places, constantly on the move,
Who will carry my letters home?

Gathering edible greens, oh gathering edible greens,
The sprouts of greens have grown old.
Saying "return home," oh, the road back home,
In the blink of an eye, another half year has passed.
Official duties for the state are never-ending,
Yearning for rest, but it's elusive.
My heart aches as if simmered in oil,
I wonder if I'll ever return home!

What are those blossoms in full bloom?
They are the beautiful tangdi flowers.
Whose chariot is this?
The general rides in it for battle.
The chariot is ready to depart,
Pulled by four strong horses.

In times of war, there's no room for stability,
For a month, we'll defeat the enemy with might.

Driving a chariot with four powerful stallions,
Strong and towering, these steeds.
The general commands from the chariot,
And the soldiers rely on it for cover.
Four strong horses move forward,
Soldiers wield arrows and carved bows.
Always on high alert,
Facing the urgent threat from the Xiongnu.

In the past, I went to war on the battlefield,
Amidst the willow trees and lovely spring.
Today, returning along the journey,
Heavy snow falls, filling the sky.
The road is muddy, progress is slow,
Thirsty and hungry, enduring hardships.
My heart is filled with sorrow and grief,
Who would understand the pain in my heart?

SETTING OUT IN CHARIOTS (出车)

I ride in my war chariot,
Arriving in the outskirts of the city.
Sent from the Emperor's residence,
To this place I have been summoned.
Summoning the chariot's skilled warriors,
Quickly loading their weapons.
In this time of national peril,
Urgent matters brook no delay.

I ride in my war chariot,
Arriving in the outskirts of the city.
The chariot is adorned with turtle-shell and snake banners,
The pennants and bull tails fly high.
Also, the majestic falcon banners,
Fluttering proudly in the wind.
Worries about the impending battle weigh on my heart,
My attendants look weary and worn.

By the King's command, I am the Southern General,
Heading northward to build a fort.
The chariot rolls with a resounding sound,
The military flags unfurl brightly.
The Emperor has given me orders,
To build a fort in the northern frontier.
Renowned is my name, Southern General,
To sweep the Xiongnu out of our land.

In the past, I ventured north from my hometown,
The millet and sorghum bloomed, their fragrance filling the air.
Now our forces return along this path,
Amidst heavy snow, mud and mire.

The nation faces numerous calamities and hardships,
Daily we toil without respite.
Do we not long to return home?
But military orders are hard to disobey.

In the grass, grasshoppers chirp incessantly,
In the fields, locusts leap and hop.
I haven't yet seen the Southern General's face,
Anxiety and worries swirl in my mind.
Now that I've seen the Southern General's face,
My mood calms, no longer restless.
Renowned is my name, Southern General,
We've already cleared out the Western Rong.

Spring has arrived, the days grow longer,
Grass and trees thrive, green and lush.
Warblers sing merrily from the branches,
Maidens busy themselves gathering herbs.
We interrogate prisoners and record our victories,
Returning home triumphant to our hometown.
Renowned is my name, Southern General,
Bringing peace to the Xiongnu, prosperity restored.

THORNY PEAR TREES (杕杜)

A thorny pear tree grows by the roadside,
With abundant fruit hanging from its branches.
The nation's war never ceases,
The days of service grow longer.
Time has now reached the end of October,
In women's hearts, there is much sorrow.
Soldiers, when you have the opportunity, return home.

A thorny pear tree grows by the roadside,
With lush leaves and strong branches.
The nation's war never ceases,
My heart is truly sad.
Wild grass and trees are so verdant,
In women's hearts, there is much worry.
Hoping for the soldiers to return home soon.

Climbing the high slopes of the northern mountain,
Gathering the red goji berries.
The nation's war never ceases,
I worry, and my parents are heartbroken.
The sandalwood war chariot is now in disrepair,
The four warhorses are weary.
Soldiers, you should return soon!

I have not seen the returning warriors,
Anxiously I think and worry.
The promised return date has passed,
This makes my heart even heavier.
We've consulted the tortoise shells and divination,
Both say the return is not too far off,
The soldiers will be back home soon!

FISH DELIGHTS (鱼丽)

The fish dive into the fish basket,
With delicious sturgeon and shark.
At the royal banquet, there's wine,
The flavors are rich and varied.

The fish dive into the fish basket,
With fresh carp and eel.
At the royal banquet, there's wine,
Plenty of fine wine, clear and fragrant.

The fish dive into the fish basket,
With plump catfish and colorful koi.
At the royal banquet, there's wine,
Sweet and fragrant, a variety to enjoy.

The feast is so lavish,
And so delicious!

The feast is so sweet,
And so complete!

The feast is so abundant,
And perfectly timed!

FISH IN THE SOUTH (南有嘉鱼)

In the South, there are fresh and fine fish,
A group of fish swim, tails swaying.
At the royal feast, there's fine wine,
Distinguished guests joyfully raise their cups.

In the South, there are splendid fish,
A school of fish play in the water.
At the royal banquet, there's fine wine,
Noble guests drink in great happiness.

In the South, there are curved branches,
Sweet gourds climbing the tree trunks.
At the royal feast, there's fine wine,
Distinguished guests drink with relaxed hearts.

Partridges flutter through the sky,
Gathering on the trees from all directions.
At the royal banquet, there's fine wine,
Noble guests joyfully toast with full cups.

SOUTHERN MOUNTAINS AND TERRACES (南山有臺)

At the southern mountain peak, the grass is lush,
At the northern hillside, mugwort thrives.
These joyful noblemen,
Are the foundation of the nation.
These joyful noblemen,
Wish for endless longevity!

At the southern mountain peak, mulberry trees grow tall,
At the northern hillside, poplar trees are robust.
These joyful noblemen,
Are the nation's glory.
These joyful noblemen,
Wish for boundless longevity!

At the southern mountain, lush wolfberries abound,
At the northern hillside, there are plentiful plums.
These joyful noblemen,
Are revered by the people like parents.
These joyful noblemen,
Have a reputation that spreads far and wide!

At the southern mountain, strong oaks grow,
At the northern hillside, the Chinese pistache thrives.
These joyful noblemen,
How can they not have long and healthy lives?
These joyful noblemen,
Spread their good names far and wide!

At the southern mountain, fruitful jujube trees thrive,
At the northern hillside, bitter olives abound.
These joyful noblemen,
How can they not have long and healthy lives?

These joyful noblemen,
Bless their descendants with eternal prosperity!

SWEET-SCENTED HERBS (蓼蕭)

Sweet-scented herbs grow tall and long,
Dewdrops glisten on the leaves.
Since I've seen the King of Zhou,
My heart feels truly content.
We drink and chat with joy,
Everyone is happy and at ease.

Sweet-scented herbs grow tall and long,
Dewdrops on the leaves are dense and bright.
Since I've seen the King of Zhou,
I feel favored and honored.
Your virtue is impeccable,
Wishing you boundless longevity.

Sweet-scented herbs grow tall and long,
Dewdrops on the leaves are moist and bright.
Since I've seen the King of Zhou,
I'm exceptionally joyful and delighted.
Like brothers with deep affection,
Your virtues are flawless, may you have long life.

Sweet-scented herbs grow tall and long,
Dewdrops on the leaves are thick and lush.
Since I've seen the King of Zhou,
Exquisite horse trappings adorn the bronze.
The phoenix bells chime melodiously,
Countless blessings return to the virtuous ruler.

DEWY MORNING (湛露)

In the early morning, the dew is heavy,
The sun hasn't risen to evaporate it.
Such a grand banquet,
I won't go home without getting drunk.

In the early morning, the dew is heavy,
Adorning the lush grass.
Such a grand banquet,
Held at the ancestral temple, truly splendid.

In the early morning, the dew is heavy,
Drenched on the wolfberries and sour jujubes.
Noble and upright gentlemen,
Each with a good reputation.

TALL YEW TREES (彤弓)

The red carved bow's string is loosened,
Prized and carefully kept by the nobles.
I have these esteemed guests,
My heart is truly content.
The bells and drums are ready,
Early in the morning, we set up the feast and offer wine.

The red carved bow's string is loosened,
Received with honor and stored at home by the nobles.
I have these esteemed guests,
Deep inside, I'm delighted.
The bells and drums are ready,
Early in the morning, we're busy urging the wine.

The red carved bow's string is loosened,
Stored away in the storage bag by the nobles.
I have these esteemed guests,
Deep inside, I'm exuberant.
The bells and drums are ready,
Early in the morning, we're busy toasting with wine.

LUSH GREEN RUSHES (菁菁者莪)

Lush and abundant, embracing mother mugwort,
Growing in the central part of the valley.
Since I've seen those virtuous gentlemen,
My mood is joyful, setting a good example.

Lush and abundant, embracing mother mugwort,
Growing on the sandy banks in the water.
Since I've seen those virtuous gentlemen,
My heart is full of delight.

Lush and abundant, embracing mother mugwort,
Growing on the uneven hills.
Since I've seen those virtuous gentlemen,
They have given me a thousand shells as gifts.

JUNE (六月)

In June, we set out for battle without rest,
Chariots are prepared and equipped.
Four sturdy horses, strong and robust,
Carry military equipment on their backs.
The Xiongnu's arrogance is particularly brash,
Our army hurries to engage in combat.
By the King of Zhou's command, we march to conquer,
To save our kingdom and protect our king.

Four black horses are chosen,
Expertly trained and following the regulations.
In this scorching June weather,
We are well-prepared for battle.
Prepared for battle, we march urgently,
Thirty miles to the borderlands.
Following the King of Zhou, we go on a campaign,
Aiding the Son of Heaven in protecting the nation.

Four tall horses, long and strong,
Large heads and powerful bodies, with a proud air.
Fiercely attacking the Xiongnu,
We build fame and renown.
The generals are strict in their military discipline,
Working together to defend the border.
Working together to defend the border,
Ensuring the stability and well-being of the nation.

The Xiongnu are fierce and not weak,
We seize the opportunity to prepare for battle.
Our target is Gaodi and Fengdi,
We've advanced deep into Jingyang.
Our army's flag waves high,
The white pennants are bright and gleaming.

We have ten large war chariots,
Boldly facing the enemy in battle.

Our war chariots are safe and sound,
Steady in all aspects, both high and low.
The four sturdy horses move in unison,
Their gait is coordinated and well-trained.
Fiercely attacking the Xiongnu,
We strike fear into their hearts.
The wisdom of the general, Yin Jifu,
Serves as an excellent example for all nations.

We invite Yin Jifu to a joyful banquet,
Finally, the Son of Heaven rewards him generously.
"I've returned from Gaodi to my hometown,
The days of campaigning have been long."
We pour the fine wine and toast to our friends,
The steamed turtles and roasted carp are delicious.
Who else is present at the feast?
The filial and loyal Zhang Zhong is also in attendance.

HARVESTING WILD RICE (采芑)

Harvesting the fresh and tender bitter wild rice,
In the cultivated fields from last year,
In these newly tilled fields.
Lord Fang personally arrives at the frontline,
With three thousand chariots lined up,
Armed and ready, awaiting battle.
Lord Fang leads the charge to the south,
Four strong and vigorous horses,
Marching forward in disciplined unison.
The general's grand chariot shines brightly,
With fish-scale quivers and bamboo blinds,
Elaborate tassels and golden bits jingling.

Harvesting the fresh and tender bitter wild rice,
In the cultivated fields from last year,
In these rural villages everywhere.
Lord Fang personally takes command,
With three thousand chariots lined up,
The turtle, snake, and dragon flags gleaming.
Lord Fang leads the troops to the battlefield,
With decorated chariot wheels and beams,
Eight phoenix bells chiming melodiously.
Official robes bestowed upon him,
Red knee guards shining brilliantly,
Green pendants tinkling melodiously.

Swiftly soaring like eagles and falcons,
Flying straight into the sky,
Resting atop the tree's peak.
Lord Fang receives orders at the frontline,

Leading three thousand chariots,
Fully armed and ready for battle.
Lord Fang leads the troops to the frontline,
Bell ringers and drummers conveying orders,
In orderly formations, they await mobilization.
Lord Fang rewards and punishes with fairness,
The drums resounding loudly, shaking the heavens,
The army presenting a disciplined front.

The southern barbarians from Jingzhou are foolish,
They dare to provoke a feud with a great nation.
Lord Fang, originally one of our elders,
Displays grand strategies and executes them.
Lord Fang leads the troops to the south,
Questioning captives and recording their merits.
The chariots race forward with a thunderous sound,
Resounding like thunder and lightning strikes.
Lord Fang rewards and punishes with fairness,
Having conquered the Xiongnu,
The southern states are left in awe.

CHARIOT ATTACK (车攻)

My hunting chariot is well-prepared,
My horses move in coordinated steps.
Four sturdy horses with heads held high,
Driving the chariot towards the east.

The hunting chariot has been repaired,
Four sturdy horses, strong and tall.
Heading to the fields with abundant grass,
Driving the hunting chariot for winter hunting.

King Xuan leads us on the hunt,
The soldiers report loudly, their voices high.
Raising turtle, snake, and cow-tail flags,
We encircle and capture game in Zheng'ao.

The nobles drive their four-horse chariots,
Four horses moving smoothly and lightly.
Crimson knee guards and golden boots,
They hunt with style and elegance.

Finger rings, arm guards, all properly worn,
Strong bows and sharp arrows, fully equipped.
The archers gather together,
Collecting the game into a pile.

Four yellow horses are well-harnessed,
The two side horses in perfect alignment.
Four horses gallop together,
Each arrow fired hits its mark.

The warhorses neigh loudly,
The flags and banners flutter in the wind.
Infantry and charioteers are vigilant,
A pile of game fills the king's kitchen.

After the king's hunt, we return to the capital,
Only the sound of chariots and horses is heard.
This sincere and virtuous king,
Has achieved great success together with us!

AUSPICIOUS DAYS (吉日)

On the auspicious day of Wuchen, it's excellent,
We offer sacrifices to our horse ancestors and pray.
The chariots for field hunting are fully prepared,
Four strong horses stand tall.
Driving the chariot up to the large earthen mound,
Chasing after herds of animals, they run quickly.

On the auspicious day of Gengwu, it's excellent,
The horses for hunting have all been selected.
Searching for the gathering place of wild beasts,
Groups of deer gather in an astonishing sight.
Driving them to the waters of Qiju,
We arrive at the royal hunting grounds.

Looking out across the vast plains,
The land is wide and rich in resources.
Running fast and slow, the animals are plentiful,
Herds and groups roam in all directions.
They all want to be in the presence of the king,
Delighted to witness the king's skill.

We've drawn our bowstrings taut,
Arrows held firmly in our hands.
One arrow pierces a small wild boar,
With effort, one arrow pierces a large rhinoceros.
The game will be used to entertain guests,
Sharing a feast and drinking wine together.

WILD GEESE (鸿雁)

The great geese soar towards distant lands,
Spreading their wings with a rustling sound.
Envoys receive orders to travel far,
Roaming far and wide, toiling endlessly.
Providing relief for the impoverished,
The widowed and orphaned, it brings sorrow.

The great geese soar towards distant lands,
Pausing to rest in the middle of the marsh.
Envoys oversee the construction of houses and walls,
The people come together to build a hundred fences.
Although everyone works tirelessly,
Eventually, they have homes to live in.

The great geese soar towards distant lands,
Crying out in lament with a mournful sound.
Only these sensible individuals,
Recognize my hardships, acknowledging my busyness.
Only those foolish individuals,
Accuse me of self-promotion.

COURTYARD TORCH (庭燎)

What time is it now in the night?
It's still early, no sign of dawn,
The courtyard torches burn brightly.
Lords and ministers gather here,
Their arrival sounds like ringing bells.

What time is it now in the night?
It's still early, no sign of dawn,
The courtyard torches shine brightly.
Lords and ministers are arriving,
Their arrival sounds like clanging bells.

What time is it now in the night?
Night is almost over, and dawn approaches,
The courtyard torches still burn brightly.
Lords and ministers are coming,
Seeing the banners waving high.

THE RIVER MIAN (沔水)

The river flows in winding patterns,
Eastward it flows, merging into the sea.
Eagles and hawks swiftly soar,
Sometimes soaring high, sometimes descending.
Alas, my brothers and friends,
Alas, the people from my hometown.
Amidst the chaos, no one cares,
Who doesn't have parents?

The river flows in winding patterns,
Vastly and mightily towards the east.
Eagles and hawks swiftly soar,
Sometimes flying level, sometimes soaring high.
Consider those who disregard the law,
Standing uneasily, I am at a loss.
Inner troubles and sorrows,
Cannot be dispelled, cannot be forgotten.

Eagles and hawks swiftly soar,
Glide along the hills and ridges.
People incessantly spread rumors,
Absurdities impossible to restrain.
Warn my friends to be cautious,
Slander is thriving and hurts people.

THE CRANES ARE CALLING (鹤鸣)

Nine winding turns, the swamp echoes with crane calls,
Their voices resounding, reaching the countryside.
Fish lurk deep in the waters,
At times swimming in the shallow marshes.
I love the beautiful large garden,
Sandalwood trees growing tall,
Leaves falling, carried by the wind.
In the distant mountains, there are precious stones,
With them, jade can be carved.

Nine winding turns, the swamp echoes with crane calls,
Their voices resounding, reaching the clouds.
Fish swim near the small islets,
At times diving into the deep waters.
I love the beautiful large garden,
Sandalwood trees growing tall,
Below the trees, there's small paper mulberry.
In the distant mountains, there are precious stones,
Likewise, they can be carved into jade.

PRAYING TO THE FATHER (祈父)

You, the one in charge of military and government, O
Father Qifather!
I was originally a warrior guarding the royal family.
Why have you sent me to this place of suffering?
Causing me to have no stable abode!

You, the one in charge of military and government, O
Father Qifather!
I was originally a guardian of the royal family.
Why have you sent me to this place of suffering?
Causing me to have no resting place!

You, the one in charge of military and government, O
Father Qifather!
You are truly foolish to the extreme.
Why have you sent me to this place of suffering?
Leaving me with no parents to honor.

THE WHITE HORSE (白驹)

The bright and pure white horse,
Is eating the tender bean sprouts in my garden.
The reins are securely fastened, hindering its movement,
Staying in my house until this morning.
For the person who is virtuous and wise,
Please stay here and enjoy yourself.

The bright and pure white horse,
Is eating the tender bean leaves in my garden.
The reins are securely fastened, hindering its movement,
Staying in my house until this evening.
For the person who is virtuous and wise,
You are a welcome and cheerful guest.

The bright and pure white horse,
Has arrived swiftly at my home.
For the sake of the public and the nobles,
Do not overstay your welcome.
Enjoy leisure without going to extremes,
Do not avoid the world, seek some relaxation.

The bright and pure white horse,
In this open and vast mountain valley,
A bundle of green grass serves as food,
Such a person, like jade, is pure without flaws.
After your departure, do not forget to send a message,
Intentions of estrangement are not those of close friends.

YELLOW BIRD (黄鸟)

Yellow bird, oh, yellow bird,
Do not perch on the mulberry tree,
Do not peck at my corn and grains.
The people in this place,
Are not kind to me.
Better return quickly,
Back to my hometown.

Yellow bird, oh, yellow bird,
Do not perch on the mulberry tree,
Do not peck at my red sorghum.
The people in this place,
Lack integrity in their dealings.
Better return quickly,
Back to my brothers.

Yellow bird, oh, yellow bird,
Do not perch on the oak tree,
Do not peck at my millet and barley.
The people in this place,
Cannot live in harmony.
Better return quickly,
Back to my uncles and aunts.

I WALK IN THE WILDERNESS (我行其野)

Walking on a desolate and lonely road,
Beside the road, the Chinese Toon trees have sparse leaves.
It's all because of the bonds of marriage,
That I am living together with you.
If you don't treat me well,
I will return to my homeland.

Walking on a desolate and lonely road,
Collecting wild vegetables is so exhausting.
It's all because of the bonds of marriage,
That I am staying at your place.
If you don't treat me well,
I will return to my family.

Walking on a desolate and lonely road,
Gathering ferns to ease my hunger.
You completely forget our past love,
Pursuing new lovers, which is detestable.
It's not because her family is wealthier,
But because of your change of heart.

SIGAN (斯干)

Flowing waters, clear and pure in the stream,
Deep and serene in the southern mountains.
Lush green bamboo, scattered in patches,
Abundant green pines stretching endlessly.
Brothers of the same lineage,
Bound by mutual friendship and love,
We do not calculate or deceive.

Inheriting the great legacy of our ancestors,
Building a thousand chambers and halls.
Doors facing west or south,
Providing stability and security in residence,
We laugh and talk, enjoying family happiness.

Tightening and creaking, the planks and boards sound,
Effortlessly packing the earth with a thump.
From now on, no worries about rain or wind,
Birds, beasts, and mice have all fled,
Only virtuous men can live here in peace.

The new palace stands upright like a giant,
Walls are neat as arrows flying.
The rooftop resembles a bird spreading its wings,
Radiant like a pheasant in flight.
The king ascends the steps with joy.

The courtyard is spacious and level,
Columns straight and towering high.
During the day, it's bright and wide,
At night, it's dim and tranquil.

Only virtuous men can live here in tranquility.

On the reed mat, we place bamboo mats,
Ensuring a peaceful and restful sleep.
Rising early in the morning, retiring early at night,
I interpret my dreams for information.
What does a good omen dream look like?
It's a dream of bears and leopards,
A dream of vipers is also auspicious.

The dream diviner says this:
Seeing bears and leopards is most auspicious,
Indicating the birth of a son.
If you dream of both large and small snakes,
It is a sign of a daughter.

If a son is born,
Dress him in fine clothes.
Let him play with white jade toys.
His cries will be vigorous,
With crimson attire, he will be splendid,
A prince or king he will become.

If a daughter is born,
Lay a mat for her to sleep on the floor.
Wrap her in a small swaddling cloth,
Let her play with a spinning wheel.
Be cautious in your speech and conduct,
Manage household chores and meals,
Do not let your parents worry too much.

NO SHEEP (无羊)

Who says you have no sheep,
Three hundred of them, on the hillside.
Who says you have no cattle,
You have ninety large cows.
The sheep descend from the hills,
Horns and hooves closely gathered.
The cattle descend from the hills,
Ears gently swaying.

Some sheep descend the slope,
Some drink by the pond,
Some walk, and some rest.
The shepherds have returned,
Wearing bamboo hats and raincoats,
Carrying sacks of provisions.
The sheep and cattle have coats of many colors,
Offering sacrifices, the variety is numerous.

The shepherds have returned,
Collecting tree branches for fuel,
Catching female and male birds.
The sheep have also returned,
Huddled together for warmth,
Not running away, their number is undiminished.
The shepherds wave their arms,
The sheep and cattle enter the pen and no longer run.

The shepherds dreamt something strange,
Dreaming that locusts turned into fish,
And tortoise-shell flags into eagles.

A dream diviner came to interpret:
Dreaming of locusts turning into fish,
Foretells a year of abundance and celebration.
Tortoise-shell flags turning into eagles,
Indicate prosperity and happiness in people and progeny.

FESTIVAL AT MOUNT ZHONGNAN (节南山)

Towering and steep, Mount Zhongnan stands,
Layered rocks and cliffs, rugged and grand.
Renowned as Lord Yin, the Chief of State,
The people all look up to your fate.
My heart is filled with anger's fiery blaze,
Afraid to speak out, afraid to raise.
The nation has fallen into decay,
Why do you still turn a blind eye, I say!

Towering and steep, Mount Zhongnan's ascent,
Sloping hillsides wide, a vast extent.
Renowned as Lord Yin, the Chief of State,
Unjust deeds, for what reason does it create?
Heaven sends disasters, unceasingly,
The nation in turmoil, the people in misery.
Public grievances are boiling, no kind word,
Why not examine your own actions, my lord?

Lord Yin, oh Lord Yin, you are the nation's pillar,
Holding the power, to make things tranquil and still.
The emperor relies on you for assistance,
The people depend on you for their subsistence.
Heavenly favor you have in your grasp,
Why do the commoners suffer hardship, alas!

You've never personally managed the state's affairs,
The people distrust you, their concerns in layers.
You don't promote the talents, nor make them serve,

230

Ignoring the righteous, you let the wicked swerve.
Quickly rectify your heart and mind,
Don't appoint unqualified kin, please be kind.
Relatives with shallow skills and petty fame,
Shouldn't be entrusted with duties and fame.

Oh, Heavenly Father, so unfair you've been,
Sending calamities to harm the common men.
Oh, Heavenly Father, so unkind you've been,
Bringing disasters to my people again.
If good people could rule the nation's helm,
Peace would return, people's hearts would be calm.
If governance were fair and just in sight,
People's grievances would cease, day and night.

Alas, Heavenly injustices remain,
Disasters keep coming, causing endless pain.
Year after year, month after month, they fall,
People's lives are restless, with woes to recall.
Worried hearts are like those suffering from drink,
Who holds the power for the nation to thrive and wink?
If the ruler does not attend to state affairs,
In the end, it's the commoners who bear the snares.

Four strong stallions harnessed and mounted well,
Strong and well-fed, their necks sturdy as they swell.
I look in all directions with searching eyes,
Unaware of where you gallop, a swift surprise.

When you are fierce and full of might,
You wield your spear, a fearsome sight.
Once your temper calms, your smile does gleam,
Raising a cup in cheers, hearts dancing in a dream.

Oh, Heaven, how unjust you seem to be,
Causing unrest and turmoil for my king to see.
Lord Yin doesn't change his wicked ways,

Instead, he resents his advisors' rightful praise.

My father composed poems to denounce and speak,
Investigating the root of our nation's bleak.
May the king's heart and mind change their tune,
For the well-being of all, under the sun and moon.

THE FIRST MONTH (正月)

In the first month, the ground is frosty and cold,
It fills my heart with sorrow, so bold.
Rumors spread among the common folk,
Buzzing and circulating, a wide yoke.
I feel so lonely and full of despair,
Worries and thoughts, my heart's heavy wear.
I lament my own timid and small,
Allowing sorrow and illness to befall.

Why did my parents bring me to life,
Only to subject me to this strife?
Disasters occurred not in my prime,
Nor after death, in some other time.
Good words flow from people's tongue,
But ill words spread, causing much wrong.
Suffering and distress are hard to bear,
Insults and scorn make it harder to bear.

Anxieties mount, my heart is not at ease,
I, with no fortune, live as I please.
The common folks, they're not at fault,
Yet they've become servants, as a result.
It's sad for us, the commoner's plight,
Where can we seek a better light?
Watching the ravens fly above so high,
Who will descend upon our rooftops nigh?

Look at the thickets, lush and dense,
Thick branches and fine grass, immense.
The common people face dangers afar,

With the sky darkening, like a falling star.
Heaven has control over all,
No one can defy its overarching call.
Oh, Heavenly God, I ask of thee,
Why does your wrath affect humanity?

Some say mountains are low and flat,
Yet in truth, they're massive, that's that.
Rumors circulate among the crowd,
Why aren't they stopped and cried out loud?
Summon wise advisors to consult,
Use dreams to discern and halt.
All claim they are the wisest in sight,
Who can tell a crow from its might?

People say the sky is vast and high,
Walking, they dare not raise their eye.
People say the earth is thick and dense,
Walking, they dare not step off hence.
People shout such words aloud,
And indeed, they are wisely endowed.
Alas, the people of this world,
Are they not like vipers, teeth unfurled?

Look at the hillsides, patches of land,
Some crops thrive with heads held grand.
Heaven sends calamities to thwart,
Fearing it won't bring me to naught.
When seeking my counsel for the best,
It's like they're afraid it won't manifest.
Once in hand, they put it aside,
Not letting me serve the nation with pride.

Heavy worries lie deep within,
As if my heart is tied in a spin.
The current state is dire and bleak,
Why is it so cruel, I speak?

It's like a raging wildfire's course,
How can it be extinguished, of course?
The mighty Zhou dynasty's fame,
Brought low by Bao Si, a foul name.

With deep sorrows weighing me down,
Rain and cold misery surround.
The chariot's laden with heavy weight,
Yet the side panels are missing, I state.
The cargo is about to fall,
When I cry, "Dear brother, help me, recall!"

Don't discard the chariot's sideboards,
Instead, reinforce the wheel's accords.
Frequent care for your charioteer,
To keep the cargo, do not fear.
Only then can you navigate the danger,
Yet you seem indifferent, like a stranger.

Fish live in ponds and waters deep,
But it doesn't mean their secrets keep.
Even if they hide beneath the tide,
The clear water still shows their glide.
I'm deeply concerned, I can't ignore,
The cruel state affairs we all deplore!

They have wine to make them inebriate,
And fine feasts to savor, celebrate.
They mingle in harmony and accord,
Their feelings shared, hearts linked with the Lord.
I, on the other hand, feel so alone,
With sorrowful thoughts that have overthrown.

Vile men have grand houses and dwellings high,
Wretched folk have grains, food to get by.
The commoners today, in poverty's snare,
Enduring disasters, with none to care.

The rich revel, laughing so bright,
While the poor remain in lonely plight!

AT THE CROSSROADS OF OCTOBER
(十月之交)

Now, it's the month of October's grace,
On the first day, in the Xinyou phase.
In the sky, a solar eclipse shows its face,
A sign of danger we can't efface.
In the past, lunar eclipses, faint and pale,
But today, a solar eclipse, a darkening veil.
All across the land, people live in dread,
As ominous signs appear overhead.

The sun and moon give us a warning call,
Their courses no longer stay with the thrall.
Lords and rulers, with no just reign,
Refuse to heed wise advisors' gain.
Lunar eclipses occurred in the past,
No disturbances in the kingdom's vast.
Now, a solar eclipse foretells unrest,
Signaling trouble, a dire bequest.

Lightning flashes, thunder roars and cries,
Heaven and earth restless under the skies.
Rivers and streams churn and seethe,
Majestic mountains crumble beneath.
High cliffs turn into deep ravines,
Profound valleys into hillside scenes.
Pity the people living today,
Facing peril in their own dismay.

The Emperor, ministers, and officials high,
The Fan clan holds power, reaching the sky.

237

Marquises and barons, they're in control,
Zhongyun manages the culinary role.
Zhu Zi serves as the keeper of the script,
Jue takes charge of horses, never to be skipped.
Yu Er presides over the education's light,
The beautiful queen reigns with all her might.

Oh, the Emperor, so wise and bright,
Didn't he know the seasons' right?
Why make me toil, without a clue,
And leave me in the dark, it's true?
Tearing down my walls, my abode so dear,
Leaving my fields fallow, barren and clear.
He claims, "I'm not causing you pain,
It's the way of the land, as the rules ordain."

This wise Emperor, so deft and shrewd,
Wants to build a great city, pursued.
He selects three wealthy men to steer,
Not one elderly minister to revere.
Not a single veteran to guard the throne,
Protecting the king and the city's zone.
Choosing the rich with horses and wealth,
Re-locating them, in search of self.

I exerted all my strength, with might,
But I dare not claim any might.
Without fault or blame in sight,
Slandered and insulted day and night.
The common folk suffer in despair,
Calamities befall, and life's unfair.
Smiles to my face, behind my back, they chide,
The wicked rule, with arrogance, they ride.

Sorrow and anxiety never seem to cease,
Painful thoughts and worries increase.
People in every direction live at ease,

But I alone remain in sorrow's freeze.
While everyone else enjoys tranquility,
I can't find a moment of serenity.
Fate's ever-changing, hard to predict,
I dare not imitate my friend's carefree habit.

RAIN WITHOUT REASON (雨无正)

In the vast expanse of the heavens so high,
Benevolence and grace rarely descend nigh.
They bring forth famine, and death they bestow,
People in all directions suffer woe.
Heaven, unfeeling, inflicts ruthless wrath,
No consideration, no foresight hath.
Those who are guilty meet a dreadful end,
Confession and justice their lives suspend.
Why should the innocent suffer such plight,
Each and every one, a grievous blight?

The Western Zhou capital's demise we trace,
Nowhere to take shelter, our hearts in a race.
Eminent ministers left the city's fray,
No one knew the hardship they'd convey.
Situ, Sima, and Sikong, you see,
They refused to serve day and night for the decree.
Princes and lords were all the same,
No willingness to exert, no desire to aim.
Hoping that King Zhou would act with grace,
Instead, he engaged in wanton embrace.

I dare to ask why Heaven above,
Doesn't heed laws and wise counsel, in love.
Like those who journey far and wide,
With no destination, no end to ride.
Amongst the ministers and noble elite,
Caution and prudence, they should repeat.
Why disregard reverence and dread,
Don't they know to fear fate's thread?

The disaster of the Dog Rong still prevails,
Famine continues, and the land ails.
Only the king's ministers, faithful and true,
Bear the sorrow, their faces askew.
Amongst the ministers and noble elite,
No one dares to advise, for fear of defeat.
The king only loves to hear praise,
He rebuffs advice, in all his ways.

Alas, we have words we dare not speak,
Not because our tongues are weak.
Words, once uttered, bring disaster anew,
Those who speak them, face trouble too.
Those who are eloquent and can persuade,
Speak sweetly, words like a flowing cascade.
Reaping rewards, their fortunes soar,
In high office, they enjoy evermore.

Some suggest I take an official's role,
But obstacles and thorns make it a toll.
If I don't follow the government's command,
I'd offend the Emperor, not what I'd planned.
If I follow blindly, without a stand,
I'd earn my friends' disdain in the land.

They advise me to return to the capital's fold,
But there's no home for me, I'm told.
Sorrow flows, tears mix with blood,
Not a word spoken, but anger withstood.
In the past, you all left the capital's site,
Who built houses for your delight?

XIAOMIN (小旻)

Heaven's tyranny knows no bounds,
Catastrophe upon catastrophe it hounds.
Misguided methods, strategies amiss,
When will this end, when's our bliss?
Good advice you do not heed,
Wicked schemes you gladly seed.
I see today's government's plot,
Profound weaknesses, a perilous lot.

The bad you discuss, but never cease,
Bringing sadness, causing unrest to increase.
When good suggestions are put to the test,
None accepted, they're met with protest.
Bad ideas, one by one, you adopt,
No alterations, no plans rethought.
I see today's government's plot,
What will become of our nation, our lot?

Divination by the tortoise shell grows tired,
Good or bad omens are not acquired.
With so many counselors and wise men near,
Endless opinions make the way unclear.
You say I speak loudly and with might,
But who dares to take on the fight?
It's like asking a passerby the way,
To find the right path, come what may.

It's unfortunate that those in power,
Do not follow the ancient sages' hour.
They stray from the righteous path,

Listen to shallow words with a laugh.
Arguing for the sake of being right,
Ignoring wisdom, their future's plight.
It's like building a house, inquires afar,
When will the house be raised, and how far?

Even though the principles for ruling vary,
There are errors and there's wisdom to carry.
Among the people, no established creed,
Philosophers, advisors, indeed,
There are talented and capable individuals,
But they are discarded, like flowing residuals.
Abandoning talent, like flowing streams,
The nation's decline becomes extreme.

I dare not take on a tiger barehanded,
I dare not cross a river without a boat commanded.
People know only this piece of wisdom, you see,
The rest is obscured, lost in complexity.
Anxiously we serve, with worries abound,
Like standing at a deep abyss, we're not sound,
Like treading on thin ice, fear holds our ground.

XIAOWUAN (小宛)

That little spotted dove so small,
Soars high in the clouds, above all.
With a heart full of sorrow, I can't sleep,
Yearning for my ancestors, memories keep.
Until dawn, I find no rest,
Thinking of my parents, I'm truly blessed.

If you're a wise and discerning soul,
Even when drunk, you keep control.
For the ignorant and foolish, beware,
A day of reckoning, beyond compare.
I implore you, be prudent and aware,
Heaven's grace may not always be there.

In the wild, soybean plants do grow,
People pick them to ward off woe.
Silkworms on mulberry leaves reside,
Wasps build nests where they can hide.
Teach your children well, impart the lore,
Inherit ancestral virtues, evermore.

Look at the skylark in the sky,
It flies and sings as it goes by.
Every day, I labor and strive,
Each month, you embark to survive.
Rise early, sleep late, work with might,
Don't tarnish your parents' name, do right.

Jackdaws caw and birds of prey hunt,
Feeding on the fields of millet, upfront.

Pity me, poor and plagued by illness,
Fearing imprisonment, my only distress.
Grabbing a handful of millet, I plea,
Can there be a better fate for me?

Gentle and humble, uphold decorum,
Like standing atop a tall tree, reform.
Nervously I look down below,
As if near a deep valley, to and fro.
With trembling heart, I tread carefully,
Like walking on thin ice, cautiously.

XIAOBIAN (小弁)

Those joyful black crows in the sky,
Return to their nests, side by side.
Everyone enjoys happiness and glee,
Only I suffer from adversity.
What have I done to incur Heaven's disdain?
What sin have I committed in this domain?
Sorrow fills my heart, beyond measure,
I know not how to find solace or pleasure.

The once smooth road is now overgrown,
Anxious thoughts, like a pestle, are sown.
Suffering fills my heart, hard to evade,
Pain and distress, like a pestle's blade.
I lie down in my clothes, heaving a sigh,
Sorrow ages me, causing me to die.
Unable to express my cares, I'm bound,
Headaches torment me, no respite found.

By the house, my parents planted mulberry trees,
Seeing the mulberries, my heart is at ease.
No one disrespects their father and mother,
No one disobeys their father and mother.
Now I can't see my father's face,
Can't lean on my mother's embrace.
Since Heaven has given me this fate,
When will my fortune change, oh wait?

In the dense willow thickets around,
Cicadas chirp with a constant sound.
Near the deep pond's water's edge,

Reeds grow tall and dense, a hedge.
I'm like a little boat in the water's flow,
I don't know where I'll drift, where I'll go.
Sorrow entwines my soul, all-consuming,
Closing my eyes, resting, never assuming.

Deer run freely, a herd they form,
Their four hooves light, a graceful norm.
Wild chickens crow at the break of day,
Seeking their mates, they chirp away.
A diseased tree grows a tumor, so dire,
Its branches wither, they all expire.
Sorrow fills my heart, a ceaseless spree,
No one knows my solitude, you see.

Seeing people chasing wild hares,
There are those who release them from snares.
Seeing dead bodies on the road they find,
Some bury them, with concern in mind.
But those with malicious intent persist,
Cruelly harming me, their target missed.
Sorrow fills my heart, an endless well,
Tears flow, I can hardly quell.

Noble gentlemen enjoy slanderous talk,
Like drinking fine wine, a jaunty walk.
Noble gentlemen show no favor,
When they hear slander, they don't waver.
They cut trees and drag them away,
Split wood with precision, each day.
They spare the slanderous and strife,
Yet they blame me for my life.

High and steep are the mountains,
Clear and deep are the springs and fountains.
Noble gentlemen, beware what you say,
Eavesdroppers may listen to your display.

Don't approach my Fish Trap Bridge with ease,
Don't open my fish basket, if you please.
I'm still not at a point to ponder,
How things will turn out, I wonder!

ARTFUL SPEECH (巧言)

Oh vast and boundless heavenly sky,
We once held you as parents high.
We've committed no sins, no wrongs,
Why does turmoil now last so long?
Heaven's wrath is quite severe,
We're indeed without fault, clear.
Heaven's anger's gone to excess,
We're truly innocent, I confess.

At first, turmoil began to brew,
Because of undue trust in words untrue.
Turmoil reappeared once more,
Due to the king believing the lore.
If the king were to show his ire,
Turmoil could quickly expire.
If the king embraced wise counsel's guide,
Turmoil would instantly subside.

The king repeatedly believed and pledged,
Endless turmoil, as a result, surged.
The king's trust in thieves and spies,
Worsened turmoil, to our demise.
Sweet words from slanderers they bring,
Further enhancing turmoil's sting.
Slanderers neglect their duty with glee,
The king's malady grows, you see.

Palaces and temples grand and tall,
Built by ancestors, standing tall.
Rules and laws were well refined,

Established by sages, designed.
Slanderers' thoughts are not concealed,
I can discern what lies revealed.
Though the crafty hare may run fast,
Faced with the hounds, it won't outlast.

The trees planted by noble hands,
Are flexible, resilient, their stance.
They can differentiate with ease,
Rumors heard from those who tease.
Superficial, deceitful, their speech is fake,
From the mouths of slanderers, they partake.
Honeyed words, their tongues can't restrain,
Their faces thick-skinned, a lack of shame.

Who is this person, pray, do tell?
Dwelling by the river's watery swell.
Without talent or courage, alas,
The root of turmoil, oh, what a morass.
Legs injured, feet swollen and sore,
Where has your courage gone, once more?
Deception and plots, a web entwined,
How many allies do you find?

WHO IS THIS? (何人斯)

Who is this person, I must inquire?
A devious heart concealed, like fire.
Why did you cross my front bridge there,
Yet my house you did not choose to share?
Whose bidding does this person heed?
Only the tyrant's words take the lead.

You and I once walked side by side,
Who has slandered me? Who would decide?
Why did you cross my front bridge to tread,
But never entered my house, instead?
Things were not so in the days of yore,
Now I see your eyes hold me no more.

Who is this person, let me inquire?
Why stand before my house like a spire?
I hear your voice, but you're not in sight,
Don't you feel remorse for what's not right?
Don't you fear the heavens up above?
Don't you feel shame, with guilt to prove?

Who is this person, I need to know?
His actions like the howling winds that blow.
Why not approach from the north or south?
Why cross my bridge, unsettling my mouth?
When you slowly walk, you pass me by,
But when in haste, you stop and apply.
If you could come just one more time,
Would it harm you or commit a crime?

On your way back, come into my home,
My heart still delights where you once roamed.
If on your return, my house you forgo,
Your true intentions, I don't fully know.
If you could come just one more time,
My heart's peace would be sublime.

Elder brother loves the bamboo flute's sound,
Second brother's reed pipe harmonies are renowned.
You and I were once like a thread entwined,
Now you fail to understand my heart and mind.
Present offerings, swine, dogs, and fowl,
Seek divine judgment for the truth to prowl.

For ghosts and specters, you bring harm and pain,
People don't see you, your efforts in vain.
Your face, in truth, should be quite clear,
But it's obscured, leaving doubt and fear.
I compose this song with good intent,
To probe and ponder, your shifting scent.

THE GOSSIPER (巷伯)

Various patterns, vivid and bright,
Woven into colorful patterns so tight.
Who is this slanderer, with heart so cruel,
A gaping mouth like a winnowing tool?
Like a star in the southern sky, so wide,
Who plotted with him? What did they hide?

Honeyed words and empty promises flow,
Crafting deceit, spreading lies we know.
I urge you to be cautious when you speak,
For soon, no one your words will ever seek.
Crafty words and lies fall from your tongue,
Deceitful whispers on the wind flung.
Perhaps for a while, some may believe,
But your treachery, they will soon perceive.

The schemer rejoices in his sinister game,
While the victim's heart fills with sorrow and shame.
Oh, Heavenly Father, please keep watch and see,
How this gossiper's arrogance runs free,
Have mercy on those falsely accused, I plea.

Who is this slanderer, please make it known?
Why stand before my home but not my own?
I hear your words, but your face I don't see,
Don't you know to feel remorse for such plea?
Don't you fear the heavens up above?
Don't you know the wrath of truth and love?

Who is this person? What can you say?

Actions like a tempest, sweeping my way.
Why not approach from north or south today?
Why cross my bridge and leave me in dismay?
When you walk slowly, I see you're here to stay,
But in your haste, you quickly pass away.
If you came once more, what harm would that weigh?

On your return, enter my home once more,
My heart still holds the joy it held before.
If you return not, your intentions unsure,
Your true feelings remain shrouded in the obscure.
If you came once more, my heart would restore,
To a state of peace it's never felt before.

Elder brother plays the bamboo flute with grace,
Second brother joins, harmonizing in the space.
You and I, like a thread, did interlace,
Now my heart and mind you cannot trace.
With offerings made, swine, dog, and fowl,
Seek divine judgment to reveal the foul.

For ghosts and ghouls, you bring nothing but harm,
People don't see you; you sound the alarm.
Your face should be clear, no need for alarm,
But you obscure the truth, causing much alarm.
I compose this song with the best of intent,
To uncover your schemes, your twisted intent.

THE VALLEY WIND (谷风)

A valley wind comes, fierce and wild,
Covering the sky, like a tempest reviled.
Recalling the days of trials we've been through,
Only you and I, together, in the tempest we knew.
Now, you've left me, uncaring, so untrue,
Abandoning me, like a heartless adieu.

A valley wind comes, fierce and untamed,
Roaring and howling, no end to be named.
Remembering the days when you held me close,
Now, you cast me away, like a forgotten rose.
Today, life is peaceful, in happiness we repose,
Yet you've discarded me, like an indifferent pose.

A valley wind comes, wild and amiss,
Only the tall mountains remain, still and crisp.
Grasses in the mountains wither and die,
Trees in the hills, leaves falling awry.
You've forgotten my virtues, my love and my sigh,
Only harboring resentment, and that's the why.

THE TALL WORMWOOD (蓼莪)

Clusters of tall wormwood, so verdant and green,
Not wormwood, but mugwort, a difference unseen.
Oh, how much toil my parents have seen,
Raising and nurturing me, their efforts serene.

Clusters of tall wormwood, not mugwort, it's clear,
But the sacrifice of my parents, I hold dear.
Raising and nurturing me, so earnest and sincere,
Their struggles and hardships, they never made it appear.

An empty bottle, devoid of wine so fine,
The large vat, ashamed, cannot redefine.
A life of misery, with no light to shine,
Death might be better, in this life of mine.
Without a father to lean on or implore,
Without a mother to love me once more.
Leaving my home with a heart so sore,
Upon my return, it feels like home no more.

My father, my father, who gave me life,
My mother, my mother, who nursed me so rife.
Nurtured and cared for, away from strife,
I wish to repay you, but it's beyond my life.

Mount Zhongnan, so tall and grand,
The fierce winds howl, across the land.
Everyone can care for their parents so grand,
Only I have lost mine, by fate's cruel hand.

Mount Zhongnan, perilous and steep,

The roaring winds never cease to sweep.
Everyone can care for their parents so deep,
But mine are no more, my grief I keep.

DA DONG (大东)

A brimming vessel of rice in the bowl,
A sour jujube wood spoon curved and whole.
The national road is smooth and bright,
Straight to the capital, like an arrow's flight.
Nobles in carriages, they speed away,
Common folks stand, observing the display.
Turning back to see the laden carts in dismay,
Tears of hardship flowing, there's no delay.

Eastern lands, some near and some afar,
All woven fabrics swept up, no matter where you are.
In the cold winter, wearing straw shoes we share,
With frost-covered ground, our feet left bare.
Frivolous, light-hearted, nobles who bear,
Traveling the broad road, without a care.
Coming and going, wealth and goods they spare,
Leaving me with endless suffering to bear.

Clear, cool springs flow from the side,
Do not wet the firewood by the waterside.
Restless and sleepless, long sighs I hide,
For the weary souls, so much is denied.
Chopping and splitting the wood is our ride,
Carrying the load, so much to provide.
The wearied soul, aching deep inside,
Deserves some rest, let life's course abide.

Sons of the East, truly pitiful souls,
No one to comfort, only assigned roles.
Sons of the West, living grand and bold,

In splendid attire, shining like gold.
Noble sons of the Zhou, tales of the hunt retold,
For private slaves' children, no warmth to hold.

To the East, fine wine you see,
To the West, it's but a simple brew, decree.
Eastern folk adorn with beautiful jade,
In the West, considered mixed stones, cascade.
In the sky, the Milky Way does pervade,
A mirror too shines, light never to fade.
The Weaver Girl constellation with grace displayed,
Moving seven times a day, no dues unpaid.

Though it moves seven times in the sky,
Patterns on the loom remain awry.
The Cowherd Star shining high,
Cannot be used to pull a cart nearby.
In the East, a bright star will lie,
In the West, Cháng Gēng, with the sun, will vie.
With a long handle, like a bird net, to the sky,
On its celestial path, it will always comply.

The Southern Dipper shines so bright,
Cannot be used to sift grain quite right.
The Northern Dipper, a guide at night,
Cannot serve as a ladle, pure and white.
In the South, the Dipper's radiant light,
Like a broad and long tongue in sight.
In the North, the Dipper's handle upright,
Morning and evening, it takes its flight.

APRIL (四月)

April, summer is drawing near,
June's scorching heat soon to appear.
Ancestors, all my kin so dear,
Why must I endure such hardship and fear?

In cold winter, winds and rain,
Leaves are falling, a barren terrain.
Separated from home, endless pain,
When will I see my family again?

In the harsh winter, chill to the bone,
Fierce winds howling, no mercy shown.
People living well, on a throne,
While I'm far from home, all alone!

On the mountains, flowers stand tall,
Chestnut and plum trees for all.
Why this suffering, this painful fall?
What wrong did I do, can anyone recall?

See that spring flows downhill fast,
Sometimes clear, sometimes it's amassed.
Troubles befall me, from first to last,
When will my days of peace be recast?

Jiang and Han Rivers, they surge and flow,
Rivers from the South to the main stream go.
I work diligently, my efforts to show,
But no one acknowledges, the hardships I undergo.

In this vast land, which plot of earth,
Is not owned by the king's royal birth?
Among the people, what's your worth,
As servants and subjects, since your birth?

Officials have orders to send me far,
Assignments pile up, like a load in a car.
They praise my youth and strengths, bizarre,
But service for my parents is still bizarre.

Some stay at home, in ease they bask,
Others for their country toil and task.
Some enjoy sleep, unburdened, they unmask,
While I suffer in a distant, foreign flask.

The mountain is full of good flowers and trees,
With chestnut and plum, the forest please.
Why such devastation, such a stark freeze?
I don't know what wrongs I've done, oh, these!

Look at the spring, down the slope it strays,
Sometimes it's pure, sometimes it betrays.
I face misfortune in myriad ways,
When will my days be free from dismays?

The Big Dipper stands high and bright,
But it can't sift grain with all its might.
The Northern Dipper, guiding the night,
Can't scoop up the wine with all its height.

In the South, the Dipper shines with delight,
Like a wide and long tongue, in sight.
In the North, the Dipper's handle upright,
Morning and evening, taking its flight.

NORTH MOUNTAIN (北山)

Climbing the northern hill so high,
Picking wolfberries as they lie.
Strong and able, my fellow kin,
From dawn till dusk, we labor within.
The king's commands, a ceaseless din,
No time to care for my next of kin.

The whole world is the king's domain,
All nations under his reign.
In this land, people feel the strain,
While I, the most toil sustain.

Four horses pull the cart in the field,
Official orders, unending and sealed.
They say I'm young, my strength is revealed,
But service for my parents remains concealed.

Some stay at home in comfort's grasp,
Some work for their country, a demanding task.
Some sleep soundly, their troubles unasked,
While I toil on, my strength unmasked.

Some enjoy the joy of fine wine,
Some worry about life's design.
Some speak of greatness, their voices incline,
Some manage every task, no need to assign.

NO NEED TO PUSH THE HEAVY CART
(无将大车)

Don't push that heavy cart along the way,
You'll only end up covered in dust all day.
Don't dwell on sorrows that won't sway,
It'll only bring more pain your way.

Don't push that heavy cart, it weighs you down,
Dust obscures the path, in shades of brown.
Don't dwell on sorrows, they make you frown,
Restless hearts breed illness, renown.

Don't push that heavy cart, it blocks your sight,
Dust clouds the road, obscuring the light.
Don't dwell on sorrows, they grip you tight,
Adding to your burdens, day and night.

XIAO MING (小明)

Bright and clear, the heavens above,
Shining on all, with boundless love.
I labor on in the western lands,
To desolate borders, following demands.
Left my hometown on a February day,
Endured both heat and cold on my way.
Heart filled with sorrow, in disarray,
Labor and toil bring pain each day.

Thoughts of family and my dear wife,
Tears flowing like rain, the pain is rife.
Do you think I don't want to return to life?
Fearful of the law's ruthless strife!

Recall those days when I enlisted,
Replacing the old with the new, life adjusted.
When can I finally return, invested?
At year's end, my hopes unadjusted.

Now I'm alone, no one by my side,
Daily chores and tasks, no place to hide.
Endless worry, sorrow as my guide,
Constant toil, no respite inside.

Thoughts of family and my dear wife,
Leaving the house, fills my heart with strife.
Do you think I don't want to return to life?
Fearful of superiors' blame, in the line of fire.

Recall those days when I enlisted,

Weather warming, just as predicted.
When can I finally return to life, admitted?
Government matters urgent, no time elided.

And now, a year has nearly passed,
Harvesting mugwort and beans, autumn at last.
Endless worries, a die that's been cast,
Seeking trouble, adding sorrows to the vast.

Thoughts of family and my dear wife,
Stepping outside, sleep eludes my life.
Do you think I don't want to return to life?
Fearful of unforeseen troubles and strife!

I advise you, noble gentlemen all,
Seek not just comfort behind your wall.
Be loyal to your duties, stand tall,
Associate with righteous men, don't stall.

The gods see your actions, big and small,
Granting you blessings, no need to install.

I advise you, noble gentlemen all,
Don't covet comfort, lest you fall.
Fulfill your duties, heed virtue's call,
Embrace the upright and righteous thrall.

The gods see your actions, they won't appall,
Bestowing blessings, ensuring you'll stand tall.

DRUM AND BELL (鼓钟)

Resounding bells, a chime, a clang,
Huai River flows, its waves unhang.
A heart filled with sorrow, a melancholic pang,
Remembering the virtuous, a memory that'll hang.

The sound of the bell, a melodious ring,
Accompanied by Huai's waters' lively swing.
My heart weighed down, troubles cling,
Thinking of the virtuous, their praises I sing.

Strike the joyous bell, beat the grand drum,
Melodies soar, three rivers hum.
Heart filled with worries, sorrows come,
Thinking of the virtuous, their virtues drum.

Golden bells ringing, a sound so bright,
Accompanied by lyres, both day and night.
Sheng and qin harmonize in flight,
With elegant music and Southern tunes so right.

Strike the bell, a sound so refined,
Accompanied by strings that intertwine.
Sheng and qin in harmony align,
With refined music, like a divine sign.

CHUCI (楚茨)

Thickets of thistles fill the ground,
Clearing fields of brambles all around.
Since ancient times, what's the goal in sight?
To plant foxtail millet and broomcorn tight.
Our foxtail millet grows lush and strong,
Our broomcorn orderly, all along.
Our granaries full, storage vast and long,
With abundant harvests, joy and song.
We use them for brewing and for meals,
To offer to gods in sacred appeals.
May the deities bless and grant us zeal.

Assistant priests serve with respect and grace,
Washing the cattle for this holy place.
Preparing offerings to their rightful space,
Some skin, some cook, with reverence they face.
Off to the ancestral temple, in their hands,
Offerings complete as tradition demands.
Ancestors' spirits descend to the lands,
To partake in the feast, as worship commands.
"Filial sons and virtuous grandsons stand,
Gods shall bestow blessings upon this land,
May your descendants thrive, vast as sand!"

Cooks prepare dishes with devotion and flair,
Laid out on the table with meticulous care.
Guests and hosts share with great fare,
Obeying the rules, speaking with flair.
Ancestors' spirits are here to partake,
With heavenly blessings at every break.

May their endless fortune be yours to make.

Our demeanor is respectful and true,
The rituals and customs we duly pursue.
A messenger to the gods, through and through,
To bestow blessings, you know what to do.
Offerings with fragrance, like morning dew,
Gods enjoy them, and hearts they renew.
May their eternal blessings find you too.

Sacrificial rites are meticulously done,
With bells and drums, as the spirits won.
The chief priest, having completed the run,
Conveys the gods' will, through the sun.
The spirits have eaten their fill, it's done,
They rise and leave as the day's begun.
The cooked dishes and offerings spun,
Taken away as the festivities shun.
Relatives gather, their hearts are won,
For a family feast, the day's not done.

Musicians come to play their tune,
Prosperity and happiness in the monsoon.
Delicious food, a fragrant festoon,
Celebrating joy, forgiving any moon.
Bellies full, moods light as a balloon,
Young and old leave, under the moon.
The spirits of ancestors and gods in tune,
Bestowing health and longevity soon.
The ceremony complete, in the afternoon,
Perfect and whole, like a sacred rune.
May your descendants inherit this boon,
With endless generations under the moon.

XINNANSHAN (信南山)

Endless, unbroken, Xinnan Mountain's domain,
Great Yu once governed, tamed the terrain.
Vast plateaus and valleys, fertile and plain,
King Zhou reclaimed, his to attain.
Setting boundaries, digging channels, his reign,
Fields squared neatly, crops to sustain.

In winter, skies are densely veiled,
Snowflakes fall, a white trail,
Combined with light rain, life sets sail,
Soaked fields, ready to prevail.
Moist earth, bountiful and frail,
Aiding crops that shall not fail.

Land demarcations, ridges defined,
Foxtail millet and broomcorn entwined,
Abundant harvests, grains enshrined,
Offered to gods, a blessing assigned.
The spirits are pleased, happiness confined,
May they grant longevity, love intertwined.

A thatched hut erected on the land,
Melon vines and crops in the sand.
Peel the melon, it's all planned,
As an offering to the ancestors' strand.
Preserve peace and life as a band,
Bless us from above, a guiding hand.

Offering the spirits pure, clear wine,
A reddish-yellow ox, to define,

Please our ancestors with grand design.
A knife so sharp, its edge aligned,
Skin removed, fur they decline,
Blood and fat, a feast divine.

Winter sacrifice, offerings displayed,
Rich fragrances, the air's charade,
Spiritual beings, by tradition, obeyed.
Spirits descend, none would evade,
"Filial sons and virtuous grandsons," they bade,
Blessings bestowed, no dues unpaid,
May endless fortune and longevity cascade.

Assistant priests complete their task,
Cattle washed for the gods to ask.
Offerings offered, as required, the ask.
Peeling and cooking, their job to unmask.
Ancestors' spirits, the feast a grand mask,
Fulfilled and complete, no questions to task.
Ancestors ascend, no need to unmask,
They taste the offerings, a worthy flask.
"Filial sons and virtuous grandsons," they unmask,
Eternal blessings bestowed, a lifelong task.

Cooks prepare dishes, with precision and might,
Laid out on the table, in the soft moonlight.
Guests and hosts gather, spirits in sight,
Adhering to tradition, everything's right.
Ancestors' spirits partake in delight,
Heavenly blessings, a sacred rite.
May they bless you, day and night,
Endless fortune, their divine light.

With respect and courtesy, we do embark,
Following rituals, nothing is marked.
A divine messenger, bringing the spark,
Blessings they bring, like a landmark.

Offerings are fragrant, like a rosebark,
The gods enjoy, their spirits embark.

FUTIAN (甫田)

A vast expanse of fertile land so wide,
Yearly yields of grains a million stride.
Taking stored grains from the past aside,
Distributing to farmers far and wide.
Through the ages, this bounty does reside.
I go to inspect the fields with great pride,
Farmers tending, with tools by their side.
Foxtail millet and broomcorn as our guide,
I pause in my tour, my questions implied.

Foxtail millet and broomcorn laid in the shrine,
A pure lamb, its coat in wool so fine.
Offered to the local and divine,
Our bountiful harvest, it's all a sign.
Thanks to the farmers' toil, so benign.
Musical instruments, a joyous sign,
Welcoming the god of farming in his prime,
Praying for rain, a blessing to assign,
To nurture our crops, keep health in line.

King Zhou comes to survey the field,
Farmers invite him with open zeal.
Bringing meals, warm and gently steamed,
The field official's heart with joy does squeal.
He beckons a farmer, the taste to reveal,
Inspecting the crops, such a hearty meal.
Fields of crops growing with robust zeal,
King Zhou delighted, no anger to conceal.
Farmers' motivation, his encouragement seal.

Harvested grains pile high as the roof's ridge,
Granaries bulge like a towering bridge.
Grain storage barns on every ridge,
Overflowing with grains, a privilege.
Foxtail millet, broomcorn, and rice,
Abundant, thanks to farmers' sacrifice.
The spirits bestow a boon, so nice,
Longevity and fortune, a virtue so wise.

DA TIAN (大田)

The vast fields are filled with crops so grand,
With chosen seeds and tools in hand.
Preparations complete, as planned,
I use my sharp plow to till the land.
Starting in the southern fields, so grand,
Planting foxtail millet and grains on this land.
King Zhou is pleased, everything is fanned.

Seedlings bloom and flower in the field,
Grains grow strong with abundant yield.
No signs of weeds or pests concealed,
Eliminating threats, a farming shield.
Even crickets and locusts we wield,
To protect our young crops and never yield.
The Agricultural God's power revealed,
Pests burnt in fire, their fate is sealed.

Thick, dark clouds fill the sky above,
Bringing rain from the heavens, with love.
Watering the public and private fields thereof,
Some crops yet to harvest, fields to remove.
Some green stalks remain, a sight to prove,
Some crops still uncollected, there's no reprove.
Some grains scattered, like a puzzle to solve,
Lonely widows gather, their hope to prove.

King Zhou arrives at the field one day,
Farmers call their wives and children to display.
Bringing meals and porridge, in array,
The field official smiles, a scene so gay.

He grabs a nearby farmer, with a voice so fey,
To taste the food, and what they convey.
Fields of young crops, their growth in delay,
The final harvest is on its way.
King Zhou is pleased, there's nothing to sway,
Farmers work with renewed energy, hurray!

The harvest yields an abundant crop,
Stacked high, like a house's rooftop.
Grain storage barns, a sight to adopt,
Like hills and ridges, in an artist's scope.
Foxtail millet, broomcorn, each in its lot,
Thanks to the farmers and their great lot.
The spirits bestow blessings, their treasure trove,
Eternal longevity, like a message from above.

GAZING AT RIVER LUO (瞻彼洛矣)

Gazing at the grand Luo River so vast,
Its waters flowing endlessly in a blast.
King Zhou arrives here, and unsurpassed,
Fortune and blessings are amassed.
Red flags flutter in a vibrant contrast,
Six divisions in order, an inspection to cast.

Gazing at the grand Luo River so vast,
Its waters flowing endlessly in a blast.
King Zhou arrives here, and unsurpassed,
His jade-adorned scabbard shines at last.
King Zhou will enjoy longevity unsurpassed,
His household, prosperous and steadfast.

Gazing at the grand Luo River so vast,
Its waters flowing endlessly in a blast.
King Zhou arrives here, and unsurpassed,
Fortune and blessings are amassed.
King Zhou will enjoy longevity unsurpassed,
His country, forever peaceful and steadfast.

GRACEFUL AND ELEGANT (裳裳者华)

Bright flowers bloom in vibrant display,
Leaves lush, in green, they sway.
Seeing you, wise and virtuous today,
My heart feels light in every way.
My heart feels light in every way,
For your reputation, we all convey.

Bright flowers bloom in vibrant display,
Bold yellow blossoms light the way.
Seeing you, wise and virtuous today,
Your talents and manners, on full display.
Your talents and manners, on full display,
Bringing joy on this festive day.

Bright flowers bloom in vibrant display,
Some white, some yellow, in the array.
Seeing you, wise and virtuous today,
Riding four horses, in grand array.
Riding four horses, in grand array,
Six reins shining, in the sun's ray.

On the left, there's someone to assist,
A virtuous person, who can't be missed.
On the right, there's someone to persist,
A talented person, by your side, exists.
Because virtuous and talented, you subsist,
Your family's fortune will surely persist.

SANG HU (桑扈)

Chirping, chirping, the Sang Hu bird sings,
Its body adorned with splendid feathers.
A noble person is often joyful,
Receiving blessings from Heaven above.

Chirping, chirping, the Sang Hu bird sings,
Its neck feathers shimmering brightly.
A noble person is often joyful,
A shield for all the world's nations.

You are a shield and a pillar,
Princes look up to you as an example.
In harmony and respect, you uphold rituals,
Receiving blessings too numerous to count.

Rhino horn wine cups, curved and curved,
Fine wine, rich and fragrant in taste.
In your interactions with others, you are humble,
And all good fortune converges upon you.

MANDARIN DUCKS (鸳鸯)

Mandarin ducks fly together in pairs in the sky,
To catch them, nets and traps they try.
Wishing longevity to noble souls so dear,
May blessings and prosperity always be near.

Resting on the fish bridge, side by side,
Beaks tucked under wings, they sweetly bide.
Wishing longevity to noble souls so dear,
May happiness and fortune always adhere.

Carriages and horses tethered in the stable,
Feeding them well, ensuring they're able.
Wishing longevity to noble souls so dear,
May joy and prosperity forever steer.

Carriages and horses tethered in the stable,
Feeding them grains and grass, reliable.
Wishing longevity to noble souls so dear,
May blessings and fortune bring endless cheer.

KUIBI (頍弁)

A deer-skin ceremonial cap, truly fine,
Why dress up in such splendid line?
Your wine, so sweet and divine,
Your dishes, fragrant and benign.
Could these be strangers here?
No, brothers, gathered near.
Climbing vines of fern and pine,
Upon the pine trees they entwine.
Without seeing the noble guest in sight,
Anxious thoughts fill the night.
Only when the noble one appears,
Joy replaces all worries and fears.

A deer-skin ceremonial cap, truly fine,
Worn with pride, a grand design.
Your wine, so sweet and divine,
Your dishes, fragrant and benign.
Could these be strangers here?
Close kin and friends, gathered near.
Climbing vines of creeping fern and pine,
Upon the pine trees they entwine.
Without seeing the noble guest in sight,
Anxieties fade, hearts grow light.
Only when the noble one appears,
Happiness replaces all doubts and tears.

A deer-skin ceremonial cap, truly grand,
Worn with grace, a noble stand.
Your wine, so sweet, tastes like no other brand,
Your dishes, fragrant, a feast so grand.

Could these be strangers here?
No, brothers and nephews we hold dear.
Like the weather before a snowfall,
A touch of frost, a chill for all.
The day of mourning approaches near,
No chance for celebration, we fear.
Tonight, let's all drink and revel with cheer,
In noble company, joy should persevere.

CHE XI (车舝)

The carriage wheels rumble as they go,
A beautiful young maiden is to leave her home, you know.
No longer hungry or thirsty, love does show,
Welcoming the bride with virtues to bestow.
Even if friends aren't here to share the cheer,
Toasting and feasting, we're happy, my dear.

On the plains, there stands a forest fair,
Wild birds perch on branches there.
A tall and lovely maiden, beyond compare,
Educated well, grace fills the air.
The banquet is joyful, hearts entwine,
Forever, my love for you will shine.

Though the wine's taste may not be prime,
You should still have a sip, in time.
Though the dishes' fragrance may not climb,
You should still taste, in this rhyme.
Even without matching virtues in this link,
Let's sing and dance, and raise a drink.

Climbing the lofty mountain peak,
Cutting down oak wood, strong and sleek.
Cutting down oak wood for fire's heat,
Leaves lush, green, and complete.
Finally, we are wedded, hearts at peace,
In your arms, my love will never cease.

Gazing up at the towering mountain's crest,

The road ahead is smooth, we're truly blessed.
Four strong horses, they never rest,
Six reins in harmony, like a musical fest.
Today, we wed, our love unleashed,
Comforting my longing heart, now eased.

QINGYING (青蝇)

Flies buzzing and swarming in the air,
Landing on the fence, causing a stir.
A calm and joyful noble soul's affair,
Don't listen to the slanderous whisper.

Flies buzzing and swarming, a noisy fray,
Perched on sour jujube branches today.
Slanderers, devoid of virtue, in disarray,
Disturb the peace, leading hearts astray.

Flies buzzing and swarming with a din,
Landing on hazel branches, causing chagrin.
Slanderers, devoid of virtue, sin within,
Undermine our love, hearts growing thin.

THE BEGINNING OF THE BANQUET
(宾之初筵)

Guests and hosts take their seats at the banquet's start,
Orderly and dignified, each plays their part.
Tableware neatly arranged, food complete,
Wine's exquisite flavor, etiquette discreet.
Drums and gongs are all set in place,
Toasting with wine at an unhurried pace.
The largest target now stands in view,
Drawing a bow and an arrow or two.
Competing archers gather, skilled and deft,
Each shot must hit the target, to win and not be left.
With the baton, a dance begins to grace,
Music from drums and pipes fills the space.
Offering our thanks to ancestors, we pay,
With proper rituals, blessings come our way.
All etiquette is followed with care,
A grand and noble scene, beyond compare.
May the spirits grant you fortune's key,
For generations to come, happiness will be.

Though the wine may not be the finest find,
Still, you should have a taste, don't decline.
Though the dishes' fragrance may not always shine,
Take a bite and savor, in this fine dine.
Even without matching virtues in this scene,
Let's sing and dance, with merriment serene.
Up the lofty mountains, we are bound,
Cutting oak wood for warmth, we're homeward bound.
Cutting oak wood for warmth, in vibrant green,
Finally, wedded to you, my heart serene.

Gazing up at the towering mountainside,
The path is smooth, in peace we ride.
Four strong horses never tire or hide,
Six reins in harmony, like a stringed guide.
Today, we wed, our love, our pride,
Comforting my longing heart, by your side.

Beneath the guests' sober veneer,
Politeness and humility they hold dear.
When sober, their demeanor clear,
Manners refined, words sincere.
But when inebriation does appear,
Light-heartedness and recklessness veer.
Leaving their seats, they roam in cheer,
Dancing and revelry, the night's frontier.
When sober, their demeanor's near,
Cautious and composed, without a smear.
But when inebriation does interfere,
Speech and actions become quite unclear.
They say it's common when one's under the sway,
To forget decorum as night turns to day.

Guests now reveal a tipsy demeanor,
Shouting and laughing, becoming keener.
Tableware and dishes tossed, no cleaner,
Dancing askew, balance growing leaner.
They say when inebriated, it's not meaner,
Errors and confusion make one a dreamer.
Hats askew, wildly they gesticulate,
Bouncing and prancing, inebriate.
When inebriated, one should concede,
For the sake of everyone, good deeds.
To continue drinking in such a breed,
Is unbecoming, a vice indeed.
Drinking, originally a fine creed,
Should maintain good conduct, that's what we need.

Every guest arrives to take part,
Some are tipsy, some alert from the start.
With wine monitors, etiquette we impart,
And record actions for historical art.
While drunkenness may not be smart,
Some say sobriety lacks a merry heart.
Don't persuade others to play their part,
Or let them act in a manner apart.
Refrain from speaking out of turn,
Refrain from words that cause concern.
Drunken speech is often fraught,
Claiming that sheep have no horn is what they thought.
Three cups in, the head is spinning taught,
I dare not encourage more to be sought.

FISH AND WATER PLANTS (鱼藻)

A group of fish amidst water plants swim,
Moving here and there, they're in a whimsical trim.
In Haojing, King Zhou's residence grand,
He enjoys life, sipping wine so grand.

A group of fish amidst water plants sway,
With long tails, they follow the watery way.
In Haojing, King Zhou's palace in the land,
Savoring wine, in delight they stand.

A group of fish amidst water plants rest,
By the reeds they find a peaceful nest.
In Haojing, King Zhou's palace, so vast,
Luxurious rooms, pleasures unsurpassed.

HARVESTING EDAMAME (采菽)

Gathering fresh and tender bean leaves with haste,
Filling square and round baskets in this place.
Princes from afar come for an audience with grace,
What will the Emperor use to grant his embrace?
Though no grand rewards are offered in the race,
Four-horse carriages bring honor to each case.
What other rewards will be showcased?
Black dragon robes with intricate patterns laced.

Beside the clear and bubbling spring's reign,
Gathering celery, its fragrance plain.
Princes from afar pay respects, not in vain,
Seeing dragon flags in the wind's terrain.
Banners of all sizes dance, a loud refrain,
The tinkling of bells, a joyful campaign.
By chariots drawn, three or four in the lane,
Princes arrive at the court without a strain.

Crimson garments cover knees and thighs,
Tied and wrapped around the legs they rise.
Attire is neat, no room for any size,
The Emperor bestows clothing, a pleasant surprise.
All the princes truly realize,
The Emperor's rewards are a splendid prize.
All the princes truly visualize,
Rich blessings and fortunes in their eyes.

Thick and strong are the oak tree's core,
Leaves are lush, and growth they store.
All the princes, their hearts adore,

Assisting the Emperor, a united corps.
All the princes, they explore,
Blessings converge, their wealth to restore.
Your subjects are refined and more,
Accompanying you to the court, they implore.

In boats of poplar, they do glide,
Tied with hemp ropes, along the water's tide.
All the princes, in joy they ride,
The Emperor bestows prosperity as their guide.
All the princes, their hearts are tied,
With blessings and fortunes, they can't hide.
Leisurely enjoying life with pride,
Their entire lives in peace will bide.

BENDING THE BOW (角弓)

Adjusting the bow, the string pulled tight,
When the string is released, it bends to the right.
Siblings and in-laws, relations so light,
Loving each other, hearts are alight.

If you distance your kin, a sorry sight,
The common folk will also take flight.
If you can guide them with words just right,
The common folk will follow in delight.

Harmonious siblings, a virtue so bright,
Amongst each other, happiness takes flight.
Quarreling siblings, with no insight,
Amongst each other, grudges ignite.

People's hearts, if they lack what's right,
Will accumulate resentment, day and night.
Accepting a title without being polite,
Selfish desires, principles out of sight.

An old horse treated as a foal's plight,
Ignoring the consequences, future isn't bright.
Like eating, only seek to satiate,
Like drinking, never mind the state.

Monkeys climbing trees, they navigate,
Like mud on a wall, they congregate.
A true gentleman guides with no debate,
Commoners naturally follow their rate.

Snow falls heavily, a winter's weight,
In sunlight, it melts, not too late.
Those in higher positions, don't inflate,
Learning arrogance, it's not your fate.

Snow falls heavily, accumulates,
In the sun, it turns to liquid state.
Evil-hearted people, their venom innate,
In this, my heart feels heavy, oh what a weight.

WILLOW TREES (菀柳)

Willow tree branches and leaves, now sere,
Don't rest beneath them, steer clear.
King Zhou's moods are far from clear,
Avoid getting close to ward off fear.
Having quelled disaster and strife, I steer,
Yet find myself exiled, far from here!

Willow tree branches and leaves, now faded,
Don't rest beneath them, spirits invaded.
King Zhou's moods are easily persuaded,
Don't hold office, it's a fate ill-fated.
Having quelled rebellion, my work unabated,
But I'm banished to a border land, unrelated!

Even if birds can fly high in the sky,
Their limit is the heavens, don't deny.
The king's intentions are perilous and sly,
Assessing such depths is difficult to try.
Having quelled disaster, my worth I rely,
Yet sentenced to a perilous place am I!

DISTINGUISHED CITIZENS (都人士)

In the ancient Western Capital, those of high esteem,
Wore fox-fur robes, their colors gleam.
Their appearance remained unchanged, it seems,
Their speech, impeccable, like well-woven dreams.
Returning to the old Western Zhou city's scheme,
Drew the gaze of the masses, a luminous beam.

In the ancient Western Capital, those of grace,
Wore straw hats with ribbons in their place.
Elegant and poised, noble in face,
Thick black hair like silk, their beauty's base.
The past's memories they can't retrace,
In their hearts, they bear a somber trace.

In the ancient Western Capital, ladies fair,
Wore ear pendants, crystals shining in the air.
Elegant and poised, beyond compare,
Yin Ji, the beloved maiden, so rare.
The past's memories, still they declare,
In their hearts, a melancholic affair.

In the ancient Western Capital, ladies admired,
Silk and satin draped, like birds they're attired.
Elegant and poised, their beauty required,
Curling hair resembling a scorpion-inspired.
The past's memories, they still aspired,
Following in their footsteps, they desired.

No deliberate ribbon, tied so high,
The ribbons were naturally, impressively nigh.

No intentional curls did their hair belie,
Their thick tresses stood tall to the sky.
The past's memories, in their hearts, apply,
Their mood is one they can't deny.

HARVESTING GREEN (采绿)

The whole morning spent harvesting green grass,
Gathered just a handful in a pass.
My hair's in disarray, quite a mess,
Hurry back home, and my appearance impress.

The entire morning spent gathering bluegrass,
Not even a single pocket did I amass.
Promised to return within five days, alas,
Six days passed, still no return, alas!

In the past, when my husband went to hunt,
I would prepare his bow and affront.
Sometimes, he'd go fishing, a peaceful stunt,
I'd prepare his fishing line, all so upfront.

What fish did he catch in his fishing spree?
Bream and white carp, happily free.
Bream and white carp, a fisher's glee,
The fish were plentiful, as you can see.

PEARL MILLET (黍苗)

Pearl millet grows so lush and green,
Nourished by the rain, a vibrant scene.
Heading south, a journey unforeseen,
Zhaobo's consolation, a caring mien.

We carry loads and pull the cart so keen,
Horse-drawn, ox-drawn, a scene serene.
Construction in Xiecheng, it's now routine,
Why not all return, let our spirits convene!

We walk on foot and ride the cart again,
Some are teachers, and some remain.
Construction in Xiecheng, it's a gain,
Why not head back home, relieve the pain!

Xiecheng's project rapidly took flight,
Guided and managed by Zhaobo's might.
Majestic and powerful, a city's sight,
Zhaobo's command, a significant rite.

The plateau and lowlands, a leveled site,
Springs and rivers, their course made right.
Zhaobo's accomplishment, what a delight,
King Zhou is pleased, the future looks bright.

SANG TREE (隰桑)

In the lowlands, the mulberry trees sway,
Leaves lush and moist, a verdant display.
Seeing my husband return today,
My heart rejoices in every way.

In the lowlands, the mulberries lay,
Leaves abundant, in disarray.
Seeing my husband come my way,
How can my heart not feel gay?

In the lowlands, mulberry trees bloom,
Leaves so green, in a dense plume.
Seeing my husband, my heart in gloom,
Words of affection, I long to resume.

I love you, deep in my heart's room,
Why not understand, in your life's resume?
Feelings of longing, hidden in the gloom,
Not a single day do I forget or assume!

WHITE FLOWERS (白华)

Fragrant white flowers bloom so fair,
Bundles of white grass, for him I prepare.
Now he's gone far, my heart in despair,
Lonely, I guard this empty lair.

Thick clouds and mist fill the air,
Moistening white grass, beyond compare.
My fate's been tough, it's only fair,
Compared to the dew, he's unaware.

The water in the river flows north and rare,
Nourishing the rice fields, green everywhere.
Singing and weeping, my heart laid bare,
Longing for him, it's more than I can bear.

Chopping the mulberry tree for fuel, I dare,
Burning it in the stove, warmth to ensnare.
Thinking of that robust man with flair,
It truly pains my heart to wear.

In the palace, the grand bell rings its glare,
Its sound echoes throughout the square.
Thinking of it makes me lose my stare,
He treats me like a stranger, it's not fair.

Ugly kites soar by the fish weir,
Elegant cranes in the forest, they appear.
Thinking of that robust man so dear,
In the blink of an eye, he's not here.

The flat and rounded stones we prepare,
Even though they're low, people tread with care.
I resent him for being so far, I declare,
His absence makes my suffering flare.

TENDER SPARROWS (绵蛮)

A beautiful little yellow bird in sight,
Landing on the winding mountain's height.
The road ahead is a daunting flight,
My weariness, I cannot hide tonight.
He feeds me and offers insight,
Guiding me through day and into night.
After commanding the cart to alight,
He instructs me to sit and find delight.

A beautiful little yellow bird in view,
Perching on a hill, so pretty and true.
Not daring to fear, but instead pursue,
Worried I won't run fast as I knew.
He feeds me, provides guidance too,
Commands the cart to make a stop or two.
Letting him rest his feet and renew,
Recharge his energy before he grew.

A beautiful little yellow bird, so dear,
Landing on the slope, not giving in to fear.
Not daring to fear, but goals kept clear,
Worried I may not reach, shed a tear.
He feeds me, gives counsel to endear,
Commands the cart to hasten, my dear.
Allowing him to sit and be sincere,
To arrive more swiftly, have no veneer.

BOTTLE GOURD LEAVES (瓠叶)

Bottle gourd leaves sway and prance,
Harvested for meals and soup, enhance.
A nobleman presents wine's expanse,
Fills the cups, invites guests to a dance.

Tender rabbit meat, so fresh to entrance,
Grilled and roasted, aromas enhance.
A nobleman brings wine's circumstance,
Fills the cups, honors the audience.

Tender rabbit meat, freshness in advance,
Roasted and grilled, flavors enhance.
A nobleman prepares wine's performance,
Fills the cups, with respect in abundance.

Tender and fresh, rabbit meat's romance,
Roasted and grilled, exquisite in stance.
A nobleman arranges wine's importance,
Raises cups in mutual admiration and trance.

GRADUALLY RISING STONE (渐渐之石)

Mountain peaks, cliffs so steep,
Soaring high, to the clouds they leap.
Through these mountains, rivers creep,
Day and night, the journey's keep.
Generals and soldiers, march and sweep,
Onward they go, no matter how deep.

Mountain peaks, cliffs to scale and reap,
High and steep, difficult to keep.
Through mountains and valleys, the path is cheap,
Not knowing when the journey's complete.
Generals and soldiers, courage and strength they reap,
Pressing forward, the dangers they face, not a leap.

White-footed pigs, neither large nor sheep,
Crossing waters, wading deep and steep.
The moon draws near, stars in a heap,
Heavy rains combine into a river's sweep.
Generals and soldiers, their commitment is deep,
Focused on their mission, in tasks they're steep.

WILLOWHERB BLOOMS (苕之华)

In the sky, willowherb blooms with grace,
Bright yellow flowers in a vibrant chase.
Inwardly, sorrow I can't efface,
Pain and sadness I embrace.

In the sky, willowherb's vibrant race,
Green leaves abundant, in their place.
Inwardly, this suffering I face,
Perhaps life's existence is a disgrace.

Big-headed sheep and fish in a case,
Reflected in the stars' celestial space.
With food to eat, we set our pace,
Never aiming to fill our stomach's base.

WHY DOESN'T THE GRASS WITHER
(何草不黃)

What kind of grass doesn't wither away?
What day isn't filled with the rush and sway?
What person doesn't march and convey,
East, west, south, north, on a constant display?

What kind of grass doesn't decay, decay?
What person doesn't face life's array?
Pity us, the ones who go and obey,
Yet not always recognized as they say.

Neither wild buffalo nor fierce beast of prey,
Often in the wilderness, they make their way.
Pity us, the ones who toil night and day,
In ceaseless toil, work without delay.

A fox's tail bushy, where it likes to stay,
Hiding in the deep and verdant array.
On a high cart, they travel each day,
Endless journey on a lengthy highway.

THE GREAT ODES (大雅)

The Great Odes consist of thirty-one poems and are musical compositions for temple ceremonies. They were composed during the Western Zhou period, and many of their authors were prominent figures in the Zhou dynasty. The content primarily praises the achievements of the Zhou dynasty's early kings and nobles, narrates the history of the Zhou dynasty, and covers various aspects of politics, military affairs, and rituals. Overall, the tone is solemn and dignified, lacking the lively and diverse style and content found in the "Xiao Ya" odes. However, the structure is well-organized, the narrative is intricate and profound, and reading them imparts a sense of reverence and depth. They are also valuable primary sources for understanding the history of the Zhou dynasty.

KING WEN (文王)

The spirit of King Wen is in the upper domain,
In the sky, it radiates brightly.
Although Zhou was a former state,
A new aura emerged in its fate.
The future of Zhou is indeed glorious,
Heaven's will cannot be thwarted.
The spirit of King Wen rises and descends,
Always by the side of the Heavenly Emperor.

With diligence and effort, King Wen toiled,
His excellent reputation spread widely.
Heaven commanded him to establish Zhou,
Generations of descendants became lords and kings.
King Wen's descendants prospered abundantly,
Main and collateral branches thrived for centuries.
All those who served as officials in Zhou,
Their generations displayed honor and glory.

Generations displayed honor and glory,
Planning meticulously for the state.
Talented and virtuous people abound,
Fortunate to be born in Zhou's land.
Zhou produced many virtuous officials,
They are the pillars of the nation.
Talents and abilities gathered together,
King Wen used them to secure the state.

Respectful and solemn, King Wen,
Righteous, bright, and dignified.

The mandate from Heaven is truly great,
Shang's descendants returned to Zhou.
Shang's descendants are many and diverse,
Countless, impossible to estimate.
Since Heaven has issued its command,
They willingly serve Zhou with loyalty.

Shang's descendants serve Zhou,
Demonstrating that Heaven's mandate isn't constant.
Shang's officials were strong, handsome, and swift,
They came to the capital to assist in the rituals.
During the ritual of libation pouring,
They still wore Shang attire.
King Zhou appointed these officials,
Remembering their ancestral virtues is paramount.

Remembering their ancestral virtues is paramount,
Continuing and enhancing their virtues.
Complying with the mandate from Heaven,
Seeking many blessings and good fortune.
When Shang still had the people's hearts,
They responded to Heaven's mandate and enjoyed their
rule.
Drawing lessons from Shang's rise and fall,
The state's prosperity is not easily maintained.

The state's prosperity is not easily maintained,
Don't let it slip from your hands.
Promote goodness and a good reputation,
Shang's example is Heaven-sent.
Heavenly matters follow a constant path,
Silent and unfathomable, difficult to understand in detail.
As long as you respect King Wen's ways,
All the states in the world will admire and respect you.

DAMING (大明)

Clearly, the ruler's virtue spreads throughout the land,
His majestic destiny shines from above.
The constancy of destiny is hard to believe,
Kings cannot easily assume their roles.
The throne originally belonged to King Zhou of Shang,
Yet, he allowed it to slip away from him.

Two noble ladies, the Rens of the state,
Hailing from a great land known as Shang,
Married into our Zhou state,
In the capital, they became brides anew.
One became the wife of King Ji,
With noble character and a renowned name.

After marriage, joyously carrying twins,
She gave birth to a wise son, King Wen.
It was this King Wen,
Cautious, diligent, and resolute.
With sincere devotion to the deities,
He brought forth numerous blessings.
His character was truly noble,
People from all directions admired and respected him.

Heavenly insight, with its radiant gaze,
Designated the mandate to King Wen.
In the early years of his reign,
Heaven arranged a marriage for him.
The bride's family resided north of the Qi River,
Along the banks of the Wei River.
King Wen admired the bride from a great land,

Praising the virtuous maiden.

This virtuous maiden from a great land,
Was like a heavenly immortal.
After the betrothal and wedding ceremonies,
King Wen personally welcomed her by the Wei River.
Connected by large boats forming a bridge,
A magnificent and renowned event.

Heaven descended with a mandate,
Commanding King Wen,
To establish his ruling state in the Zhou capital.
In the state of Shen, there was another virtuous maiden,
The eldest daughter married King Wen,
And through Heaven's grace, gave birth to King Wu.
May you protect King Wu,
And unite with the feudal lords to overthrow Shang.

Shang gathered a vast army,
Soldiers as numerous as a dense forest.
King Wu solemnly pledged in the pasture,
"We, the Zhou army, are the mightiest,
Heaven watches over you,
Do not harbor doubts or desires for glory!"

The vast pasture became the battlefield,
Chariots of tan wood gleaming brilliantly.
Four horses pulled the chariots, truly majestic.
The Chief Minister, assisting King Wu,
Like an eagle soaring high.
Assisting King Wu in victorious battles,
Relentlessly pursuing and defeating Shang,
Clearing the world of the wicked.

MIAN (绵)

Endless rows of gourds, interlinked,
The Zhou people's birthplace gradually thrived.
From the earth, they moved downstream to Qishui.
Ancient Duke of Tanfu faced challenges,
Digging pits and tunnels to shield from the cold,
Without houses, what could be done?

Ancient Duke of Tanfu diligently inspected,
Early morning, he left his home.
Following the Wei River westward,
Arriving at the foot of Qishan Mountain.
Together with his virtuous wife, Taijiang,
They surveyed and selected a site for building.

Zhouyuan, fertile and expansive,
Sorghum and bitter melon as sweet as candy.
Everyone discussed and deliberated,
Casting turtle shells to divine auspiciousness:
The divination said they could settle here,
So they built new houses in this place.

Thus, they settled contentedly in Qixiang,
Houses on the left and right were constructed,
Land boundaries were defined, fields were tilled,
Ditches dug, and soil well-managed.
From west to east, everything was uniform,
Each person responsible for their tasks, full of joy.

The Marquis of the Soil was appointed for engineering,
The Minister of Land and Labor oversaw the land.

They swiftly built new residences.
Pulling taut the cords and plumb lines,
Erecting wooden boards for the earthen walls,
A grand ancestral temple was built.

Shoveling soil, thudding into baskets,
Dumped into molds, resounding echoes,
Pounding earth, resounding thump-thump-thump,
Carving walls, resounding bang-bang-bang.
A hundred earthen walls stood erect,
The people's voices even louder than the drums.

Building the outer city gates,
The city gates were lofty and grand.
Constructing the royal palace's main gate,
The main gate was dignified and stately.
Constructing earthen altars for sacrifices,
People gathered for blessings and good fortune.

Still furious with the enemy, not yet quelled,
King Tai's reputation spread far and wide.
Oaks and chestnut trees were all uprooted,
Traffic routes were clear and open.
The Kunyi were alarmed and fled,
Breathless and exhausted, they tasted bitterness.

The states of Yu and Rui no longer quarreled,
King Wen's influence reformed their character.
I have virtuous ministers who return to serve,
I have talented advisors to aid in state affairs,
I have virtuous scholars who actively engage,
I have valiant generals to defend against insults.

YUPU (棫朴)

Yupu and Zhe trees, leaves thick and lush,
Suitable for sacrificial fires to the heavens.
A ruler of dignified bearing,
Surrounded always by his ministers.

A ruler of dignified bearing,
With someone holding jade and scepter at his side.
With jade and scepter in hand, dressed in splendor,
Noble gentlemen, their demeanor impeccable.

Warships sail on the Jing River,
Soldiers row oars, facing wind and waves.
King Zhou follows the river, setting out on campaigns,
Six armies following, majestic and grand.

Look at the bright Milky Way,
The night sky beautiful and clear.
King Zhou, healthy and long-lived,
Nurtures numerous talents.

Meticulously carving and diligently cultivating,
His qualities like precious gold and jade.
Industrious without end, our King of Zhou,
Leading the realm, safeguarding the four corners.

HANLU (旱麓)

From afar, observe the foothills of the dry mountains,
Densely covered with hazel and jujube trees.
The easy-going and cheerful King of Zhou,
With joy and ease, seeks blessings and fortune.

A bright and pure white jade wine vessel,
Filled with golden, exquisite wine.
The easy-going and cheerful King of Zhou,
Enjoys the blessings sent from heaven.

The soaring hawk extends its wings to the sky,
Fish leap in the deep abyss.
The easy-going and cheerful King of Zhou,
Fosters farsighted talents.

Offerings of clear wine to the gods are ready,
Red-colored bulls are also prepared.
With these offerings, we honor the spirits,
Praying for abundant blessings from above.

Lush oak and Yupu trees in the forest,
Used for firewood in the rituals.
The easy-going and cheerful King of Zhou,
Receives divine assistance as a virtuous ruler.

Luxuriant vines, branches growing long,
Climbing up trunks and into the treetops.
The easy-going and cheerful King of Zhou,
Does not deviate from ancestral traditions, seeking
blessings and auspiciousness.

SIQI (思齐)

Too virtuous and meticulous,
She was the mother of King Wen.
Zhou Jiang, kind and gentle,
Were all consorts of the royal court.
Taishi inherited good traditions,
Descendants flourishing, Zhou's dynasty thriving.

King Wen ruled in accordance with ancestral ways,
Ancestors' spirits harbored no grievances,
Ancestors' hearts at peace, no pain.
King Wen treated his chief wife with respect,
Loved and befriended his brothers,
Leading by example for his family and state.

Harmony and kinship within the palace,
Solemn and respectful, honoring ancestors.
In public, they scrutinized and introspected,
In private, they were cautious and self-disciplined.

Great calamities and difficulties were eliminated,
Harmful diseases among people eradicated.
They accepted good advice when heard,
Embracing counsel from sincere advisors.

Adults exhibited virtuous conduct,
Youth could also achieve great merit.
Ancient teachings passed down forever,
Selecting talents and the virtuous.

HUANGYI (皇矣)

The wise and great God above,
Oversees the affairs of mankind.
Observing all corners of the world,
Understanding the sufferings of all.
Ruling over the Shang Dynasty,
Failing to win the people's hearts leads to a dark rule.
Looking at the neighboring vassal states,
Who will bear the heavy burden of the world?

God's will is with the Zhou kingdom,
And they shall expand their territories.
So, they turn their gaze to the west:
"Here, we shall dwell in peace!"

Clearing and uprooting the weeds,
Removing dead branches and trees.
Trimming unruly branches and twigs,
And nurturing new shoots of saplings.
Opening paths through the forests and mountains,
Clearing away willows and oak trees.
Removing the bad to nurture the good,
Mulberry and yellow mulberry thrive.

God blesses King Mingde,
The Qiang Rong defeated and fleeing.
Heaven appoints him as the ruler,
Accepting the divine mandate for his dynasty.

God examines this Qishan,
Oak and chestnut trees have been removed,

A clear path through the pine and cypress woods.
God establishes the Zhou dynasty with a wise king,
Taibo and Wang Ji begin their foundation.
It is the great Wang Ji,
Understanding his father's love for his elder brother.
Loving his elder brother without reservation,
Fortune and prosperity abound.

Heaven-bestowed kingship shines brightly,
Receiving blessings and never losing them,
Possessing vast territories in all directions.

This wise King Ji,
God understands his thoughts,
His peaceful and virtuous conduct spread far and wide.
He possesses virtues, distinguishes right from wrong,
Discerns between the wicked and the good,
He can be a teacher for the people as a king.

As king of this great nation,
Harmony reigns from top to bottom,
Until King Wen ascends the throne,
Unmatched in virtue and goodness.
The blessings bestowed by God,
Extend to his descendants for generations.

God teaches King Wen:
Do not covet without a clear purpose,
Do not envy others' excessive desires.
Climb the high ridge to gain a better view.
The Mi people are disrespectful to Zhou,
Daring to resist the great nation of Zhou,
Invading Run and Co., acting recklessly.
King Wen became furious,
Zhou's forces mobilized to resist,
Halting the Mi people's aggression,
Securing the dynasty's longevity, Zhou grows stronger,

Prosperity spreads throughout the realm.

King Wen's great army stationed at Jingdi,
Previously, they had rested on Mi's territory.
I climbed a high ridge and looked far,
No one will ever again set foot on our hills,
These are our mountains and ridges;
No one will ever drink from our springs,
These are our springs and ponds.
Planning the land of Yuan fresh,
Moving to Qishan, facing the sun,
The place is near the Wei River's banks.
Setting an example for all nations,
The ruler of the people.

God tells King Wen:
I admire your virtues,
No harsh words or stern looks are needed,
No need for rods and sticks to govern your state.
It's as if you don't know, but you do,
Following the will of heaven is the law.
God explicitly instructs King Wen:
In matters of consultation, seek your friendly vassals,
Discuss with your brothers frequently.
Take up the hooks and ladders of assault,
Approach the chariots, rush into battle,
Conquer the Chong nation, make Zhou stronger.

Approach the chariots, charge forward,
The walls of Chong nation towering high.
Continuously capturing prisoners,
Calmly cutting off enemies' ears.
Hold rites and sacrifices,
Appease the defeated and persuade them to surrender,
The four directions and the state remain unharmed.
Approach the chariots with great vigor,
Chong nation's walls are solid and strong.

Suddenly launching an attack, the enemy can't resist,
Rooting out the enemy completely,
No vassal states dare to resist again.

LINGTAI (灵台)

They began planning to build the Lingtai,
Devising clever arrangements and plans.
When the people heard, they eagerly joined in,
And the grand achievement swiftly took form.

The construction of the platform was not rushed,
Yet the common people enthusiastically participated.
King Zhou strolled through the Lingyuan,
Where herds of deer rested in the grass.

Gentle does, strong and beautiful,
White cranes and egrets with bright plumage.
King Zhou arrived at the Lingtai's pond,
Ah, the pond was full of fish swimming and leaping.

The bell stand and the ceremonial arches were set,
The large drums and bells securely hung.
Ah, the drums and bells were arranged in perfect order,
Ah, the music within the temple was boundless!

Ah, the drums and bells resounded together,
Ah, endless joy in the temple!
The booming turtle-shell drums reverberated,
The blind musician played to celebrate success.

XIAOWU (下武)

The one who can carry on the ancestral legacy is the
Zhou nation,
    Generation after generation, they have wise kings.
    In the early days of Zhou, there were divine ancestors in
heaven,
    And King Wu became the Zhou king in Haojing.

King Wu became the Zhou king in Haojing,
Inherited generations of ancestral virtues.
His words and actions aligned with God's will,
As a king, he was trustworthy and respected.

As a king, he was trustworthy and respected,
Becoming a role model for the four seas.
He always held reverence and practiced filial piety,
For filial conduct is the way of the ancient kings.

The four seas admire King Wu of Zhou,
Respecting the virtues of their ancestors.
Always holding reverence and practicing filial piety,
He admonishes his descendants not to forget.

He admonishes his descendants to remember,
And follow in the footsteps of their ancestors.
Ah, Zhou's foundation lasts for thousands of years,
Blessed by heaven, boundless and eternal.

Blessed by heaven, boundless and eternal,
Nations from all directions come to celebrate the
prosperity.

Ah, Zhou's foundation lasts for thousands of years,
Distant lands serve as barriers.

WENWANG'S REPUTATION (文王有声)

Wenwang possessed a great reputation,
Spreading his immense fame to the four corners.
Seeking peace for the world, achieving tranquility,
In the end, his great achievements were a success.
Ah! Wenwang, wise and great!

Wenwang received the mandate of heaven,
Accomplishing glorious martial deeds.
Leading his troops to defeat the Chonghou Tiger,
And establishing a new capital in Feng.
Ah! Wenwang, wise and great!

They built walls along the old river,
The scale of Fengyi was substantial.
Not content with their own desires,
Following the footsteps of their ancestors to promote
Zhou.
Ah! Everyone praises King Wen!

King Wen's accomplishments were truly magnificent,
Like the towering walls of Fengyi.
Lords from all directions came together,
Supporting the realm under the heavenly roof.
Ah! Everyone praises King Wen!

The Feng River flows leisurely to the east,
The great Yu left behind tremendous achievements.
Lords from all directions came together,
Wuwang is a role model for all.
Ah! Glorious King Wu's fame shines!

The secondary palace was established in Haojing,
People from all over, west to east,
From south to north, all gathered,
No one dared to oppose Zhou.
Ah! Glorious King Wu leaves behind a great name!

King Wu divined and inquired about fortune and misfortune,
Whether to establish a new capital in Haojing.
The decision to move the capital was determined by the turtle-shell divination,
And the construction of the new capital was accomplished by King Wu.
Ah! King Wu, wise and great!

On the banks of the Feng River, the millet grass thrived,
Could King Wu really be idling about?
He left behind a strategy for the well-being of the people,
Protecting his descendants and the prosperity of the nation.
Ah! Great and wise King Wu!

THE BIRTH OF THE PEOPLE (生民)

Who were the ancestors of the Zhou clan?
Her name was Jiang Yuan.
How were the ancestors of the Zhou clan born?
Prayers to the heavens and offerings to the spirits,
Seeking to have children and continue the lineage.
Following the footsteps of the Emperor, she conceived,
Taking care of herself for a healthy pregnancy.
For ten months, she carried herself with dignity,
Gave birth to a son and became a busy mother,
He was none other than King Houji of Zhou.

Carrying the pregnancy to full term,
She gave birth to a plump baby boy.
Without any tears or ruptures,
Safe and sound, in good health,
A miraculous birth, far from ordinary.
Fearing that the gods might be displeased,
She hurriedly made offerings for good fortune,
Though she had given birth to a son, she dared not raise
him.

She left him in an alley,
Cows and sheep cared for him and fed him.
She left him in a grove of trees,
Coincidentally, someone came to cut wood.
She left him on the cold ice,
Birds spread their wings to protect him.
Later, the birds flew away,
And Houji cried loudly and incessantly,
His crying was long and resounding,

Passersby stopped in their tracks.

Houji had just learned to crawl,
Appearing intelligent and obedient,
His little mouth could find food.
As he grew older, he could plant beans,
Bean sprouts grew lush and healthy.
He planted stalks and grains,
Wheat and barley thrived without weeds,
There were also abundant melons.

Houji knew how to cultivate crops,
He had a good method of production.
Caring for the seedlings, diligently weeding,
Selecting good seeds for early planting.
The seeds broke through the soil with tender shoots,
The seedlings grew strong and tall.
They formed nodes, bore ears, and produced grains,
The grains were plump and of good quality.
The ears of grain were heavy, yielding a high harvest,
Bringing joy to the fields of Taishi.

Heaven granted excellent seeds,
Including millet, wheat, and barley,
As well as hemp, rice, and sorghum.
Millet, wheat, and barley flourished everywhere,
And during the harvest season, there was much work.
Hemp and sorghum covered the fields,
Carried on their backs and brought home,
Upon returning, they began the ritual offering.

What does the offering ceremony look like?
Some pound or scoop the rice,
While others sift the millet and barley husks.
The sound of rice washing is crisp and clear,
Steamed rice emits a fragrant aroma.
The ritual offering is discussed together,

Burning fat and aromatic herbs for a pleasant scent.
A ram is slaughtered, and its skin is stripped,
Roasted and cooked to be offered to the gods,
Praying for prosperity in the coming year.

I put the offerings in wooden bowls,
Wooden bowls filled with meat and pots filled with soup,
The aroma wafts through the entire hall.
God descends to taste,
The food is truly fragrant.
Houji initiated the ritual offering,
Thankfully, there were no disasters,
And the tradition continues to this day.

REEDS (行葦)

Clusters of reeds grow along the road,
Do not let cattle and sheep trample them.
The tender buds have just formed,
Their leaves are delicate and just beginning to grow.
Warm and close with many brothers,
Do not alienate each other; gather together.
Some set up a feast for their brothers,
Some provide seats and tables for their brothers.

Prepare the wine and dishes, set the table,
Servants take turns providing seats for the guests.
The host pours wine, and the guest reciprocates,
Cups are washed and filled again, creating intimacy.
Juices and sauces are offered,
Grilled and roasted meats are arranged.
Delicacies of a hundred kinds and beef tongue,
Stringed instruments and drums play endlessly.

The strong and sturdy carved bows,
Four arrows of equal weight and balance;
Each person shoots an equal number of times,
The guests rank and discuss their skills.
The carved bows are drawn to full capacity,
Hands hold four arrows with skill.
Four arrows simultaneously hit the target,
The ranking loser should not be underestimated.

The great-grandson serves as the host,
Offering sweet wine that is both delicious and mellow.
Filling a large cup with wine,

Praying for people to enjoy long lives.
Old age and advanced years bring good fortune,
Assisted by someone, they walk and guide.
Longevity and old age are cause for celebration,
Heaven bestows great blessings upon the elder.

ALREADY DRUNK (既醉)

Drinking wine, thoroughly intoxicated,
Your virtues are truly touching.
A nobleman enjoys a thousand years of life,
Praying for even greater blessings.

Drinking wine, thoroughly intoxicated,
Dishes are brought to the door.
A nobleman enjoys a thousand years of life,
Praying for abundant blessings like the bright sun.

Endless blessings from the radiance,
Your virtuous reputation and praise endure.
Goodness begins with virtuous beginnings,
And the spirits offer beautiful blessings.

What do the spirits say?
Clean and pure are the offerings and vessels.
Friends come with respect to assist in the offering,
Observing proper rituals, with devout hearts.

The sacrificial ceremony is perfect,
The Son of Heaven fulfills his filial duty.
A filial son's devotion never wanes,
Bestowing prosperity on your descendants.

How will your lineage fare?
Every household enjoys abundance and peace.
A nobleman enjoys a thousand years of life,
Granting your descendants boundless blessings.

How are your descendants?
Heaven bestows fortune and prosperity.
A nobleman enjoys a thousand years of life,
Heaven grants you wives, concubines, and sons.

How are your wives, concubines, and sons?
Heaven grants you talented brides.
Talented brides for your sons and grandsons,
Bringing blessings to your posterity.

DUCKS AND SEAGULLS (凫鹥)

Wild ducks and white seagulls swim in the water,
The Lord, content, comes to drink wine.
Your fine wine is clear and mellow,
Your dishes are fragrant and appetizing.
The Lord joyfully drinks wine,
Bringing forth blessings and good fortune.

Wild ducks and white seagulls on the shore,
The Lord feasts, serene and composed.
Your fine wine is truly abundant,
Your dishes are delicious and fresh.
The Lord joyfully drinks wine,
And blessings keep coming to his side.

Wild ducks and white seagulls on the shore,
The Lord feasts, delighted in his heart.
Your fine wine is crystal clear,
Your dried meat is sweet and savory.
The Lord joyfully drinks wine,
And blessings quietly approach him.

Wild ducks and white seagulls in the bay,
The Lord feasts in the ancestral temple.
Since the feast is held in the ancestral temple,
Blessings and fortunes both arrive.
The Lord joyfully drinks wine,
And blessings steadily accumulate.

Wild ducks and white seagulls by the water,
The Lord is thoroughly intoxicated.

The aroma of fine wine is delightful,
Grilled and roasted meat smells fragrant.
The Lord joyfully drinks wine,
Disasters will not visit his doorstep.

FALSE HAPPINESS (假乐)

A nobleman of goodness and joy,
His virtues shine brightly and clearly.
In accordance with the people's wishes,
He receives blessings ordained by Heaven.
Heaven decrees to bless you,
Bestowing abundant fortune and the nation's prosperity.

Endless blessings beyond measure,
Descendants in the billions flourish.
Dignified and majestic, grand and noble,
Fit to be a sovereign or a king.
Avoiding faults and never forgetting ancestors,
Strictly adhering to ancient laws and codes.

Your demeanor is dignified,
Your speech is logical and clear.
Without complaints, without weariness,
You welcome the counsel of your officials.
Abundant blessings without bounds,
The four corners of the realm obey your commands.

The four corners of the realm obey your commands,
Feasting with ministers, family, and friends.
Princes and officials all attend the banquet,
The Son of Heaven is pleased in his heart.
Diligent in their duties, never slackening,
The people are peaceful, and the nation prospers.

GONG LIU (公刘)

Honest and upright is Gong Liu,
But his dwelling place is not tranquil.
Organizing fields, marking boundaries,
Collecting grain and storing it in barns.
He prepares provisions for the journey,
Filling small bags and large sacks.
Harmonious and united, they seek glory,
Arming themselves with bows and arrows.
With shields, spears, and axes in hand,
They set forth on a distant path.

Honest and upright is Gong Liu,
Busy inspecting the wild lands of Bin.
Numerous people and complex affairs,
Their hearts find peace and contentment,
Sighing long and short, sweeping away all worry.
Sometimes ascending small hills,
Sometimes descending onto the plains.
What adorns his person?
Beautiful jade and gemstones shine bright,
His jade-handled knife is truly exquisite.

Honest and upright is Gong Liu,
Arriving at the banks of a hundred springs.
Gazing at the vast and wide plains,
Climbing hills in the southern distance,
He discovers a favorable location for the capital.
The fields around the capital are expansive,
So they settle and establish a new state,

Preparing to build new houses,
Where everyone contributes their ideas,
And they all engage in collective planning.

Honest and upright is Gong Liu,
Settling in the vast plains of the capital.
The people quickly and orderly,
Gather at the banquet hall to celebrate.
Guests and hosts take their seats,
First, they offer sacrifices to the pig deity for good
fortune.
A plump pig is led out from the pen,
Gourds and ladles scoop fragrant wine.
Everyone drinks and feasts on meat,
And they choose Gong Liu as their leader.

Honest and upright is Gong Liu,
Expanding the vast land of Bin.
Observing the shadow on the high hill,
Busy with surveys in the south and north.
Determining water sources and their courses,
The army divides into three shifts,
Measuring the lowlands for cultivation,
Opening up fields for abundant grain.
Then they go to the west to survey,
Confirming the vast expanse of Bin.

Honest and upright is Gong Liu,
Building houses on the expansive plains of Bin.
Crossing the Wei River to quarry stones,
Collecting grinding stones and ore.
Strengthening the foundations securely,
Prosperity and abundance bring joy and laughter.
Living on both sides of the Huangjian,
Gazing across to the other side of the river.
Immigrants settle in great numbers,
Continuing to reside at the Ruishui Bay.

QUAFFING THE BROOK (泂酌)

Fetching water from the distant brook,
Drawing it and pouring it into a jar,
Cooking meals with a delicious taste.
A plain and cheerful nobleman,
Like the parents of the people.

Fetching water from the distant brook,
Drawing it and storing it in the jar,
To use for washing wine vessels.
A plain and cheerful nobleman,
The hearts of the people turn to you.

Fetching water from the distant brook,
Drawing it and storing it in the jar,
To use for washing sacrificial utensils.
A plain and cheerful nobleman,
The people live in peace and hold you dear.

JUAN AH (卷阿)

Rolling hills twist and turn,
A whirlwind blows in from the south.
A plain and cheerful king,
Visits this place to enjoy and sing,
His ministers offer a loud and clear song.

Leisurely and carefree, he roams and plays,
Contented and at ease, he briefly relaxes.
A plain and cheerful king,
May you live in peace for your days,
Inheriting the complete achievements of your ancestors.

Your territory and boundaries,
Vast expanses without limit.
A plain and cheerful king,
May you live in peace for your days,
You preside over the sacrifices to countless gods.

Receiving heaven's mandate for an extended time,
Fortune and blessings grant you eternal well-being.
A plain and cheerful king,
May you live in peace for your days,
Enjoying great blessings for the longest time.

Wise and talented individuals are your support,
Along with filial children and virtuous ones,
Guiding and assisting together.
A plain and cheerful king,
May other regions follow your example.

Respectful, mild, and with a dignified air,
Your character is as pure as jade and ritual vessels,
Your excellent reputation spreads far and wide.
A plain and cheerful king,
Princes from all quarters emulate your virtues.

Phoenixes soar high in the sky,
Their wings producing a rustling sound,
Sometimes ascending, sometimes perching on trees.
Numerous virtuous men gather as one,
Obeying your orders, they are busy in all directions,
The emperor is pleased and praises abound.

Phoenixes call out with a clear voice,
Atop those lofty hills.
The tall parasol trees grow vigorously,
Facing the direction of the rising sun.
The branches and leaves of the parasol tree are lush and
dense,
While the phoenixes sing melodiously.

The king's carriages are all prepared,
Many and splendid they are.
The king's horses are tall and robust,
Skillful in running as fast as the wind.
Wise ministers offer poems in abundance,
Which are collected and composed into songs.

The people are truly toiling hard,
Seeking a little bit of peace and tranquility.
Within the realm, the people enjoy favor,
Stability is maintained among the regional lords.
Do not believe in deceitful and deceptive words,
Be cautious of villains who disrupt court politics.
Restrain oppressive and corrupt officials,
Arrest those who break the law and deceive.

Comfort the myriad people far and near,
Only then can the king's heart find peace.

The people are truly toiling hard,
Seeking a bit of respite.
Within the realm, the people enjoy favor,
As the people gather together to enjoy tranquility.
Do not believe in deceitful and deceptive words,
Be cautious of political enemies who disrupt court politics.
Restrain oppressive and corrupt officials,
Do not let the people's hearts be filled with anxiety.
Remember the previous achievements,
In order to uphold the king's good reputation.

The people are truly toiling hard,
Seeking a bit of rest.
Within the capital, the people enjoy favor,
And the regional lords are stable.
Do not believe in deceitful and deceptive words,
Be cautious of those who are two-faced and cunning.
Restrain oppressive and corrupt officials,
Do not let them run rampant.
Be prudent in your own actions,
Associate with noble-hearted gentlemen.

The people are truly toiling hard,
Seeking a little bit of rest.
Within the realm, the people enjoy favor,
Vent the grievances of the common people.
Do not believe in deceitful and deceptive words,
Be cautious of wicked individuals and their actions.
Restrain oppressive and corrupt officials,
Do not let them corrupt the king's governance.
Though your age is not advanced this year,
Your responsibility is grand and unparalleled.

The people are truly toiling hard,
Seeking a bit of peace and tranquility.
Within the realm, the people enjoy favor,
And the nation remains intact with a peaceful populace.
Do not believe in deceitful and deceptive words,
Be cautious of those who scheme selfishly.
Restrain oppressive and corrupt officials,
Do not let them overturn royal governance.
The king's love for wealth and beautiful women,
Can be addressed with frank advice and admonishment.

BOARD (板)

God's actions have been abnormal,
All the people in the world are suffering.
Promises made are not kept,
Policies are formulated without foresight.
Unlawful saints have their own opinions,
Honesty is not valued, truly absurd.
Strategies are formulated without foresight,
So listen to advice, my king.

Heaven is sending down disasters,
Don't rejoice prematurely.
Heaven is unsettled, in turmoil,
Don't be proud and forget your form.
If policies align with the people's will,
The people will live in harmony and happiness.
If policies make the people happy,
Their lives will be stable and secure.

Though our roles are different,
Ultimately, we are colleagues in the court.
Now, I discuss state affairs with you,
But you don't listen and speak out of turn.
I speak about matters of state,
Don't treat it as a joke.
As the ancients said well:
Even a woodcutter can have good ideas.

Heaven is sending down disasters,
But you behave wildly and improperly.
Old man, I speak earnestly to you,

Yet you remain arrogant and conceited.
It's not that I'm confused,
You're making fun of me too lightly.
You've gone too far in doing wrong,
It's beyond repair; the nation will fall.

Heaven is angry, sending down disasters,
You should humble yourself, not be servile.
Your appearance and demeanor are confused,
Good people are silent like corpses.
The people suffer and groan,
The future of the nation is unpredictable.
The situation is unstable,
Bringing no blessings to the people.

Heaven opens up to benevolence,
Like musical instruments harmoniously responding,
Like two jade discs combined into one,
Like taking things along effortlessly.
Carrying things without any hindrance,
Guiding according to the circumstances is smooth.
Today, there are already too many rules,
Don't create new regulations anymore.

Warriors are like fences,
The people are like city walls.
A great nation is like a barrier,
A strong clan is like a main support.
Practicing virtue brings prosperity to the people,
The royal descendants are like city walls.
Don't let those city walls collapse,
Don't let them stand alone without support.

Heaven's anger should be feared,
Don't dare to indulge or be reckless.
Heaven's wrath brings disasters,
Don't dare to be careless and invite calamity.

Heaven's eyes are the keenest,
Leading you and the king to wander.
Heaven's insight is the most discerning,
Leading you and the king on a journey.

DISSOLUTION (荡)

Indulgent and wanton is this God,
He is the master of the people below.
Cruel and capricious is this God,
His decrees are biased, often changed.
Heaven gives birth to the people,
Destinies are fickle, hard to ascertain.
In the beginning, all is well-intended,
Yet seldom does it end well.

King Wen once lamented thus:
"Alas, you King Zhou of the Shang Dynasty!
So cruel and overbearing,
Amassing wealth at the expense of the people.
You have ascended to the throne,
And wielded arbitrary commands.
Heaven sends arrogant and wicked men,
While ministers enable his tyranny."

King Wen once lamented thus:
"Alas, you King Zhou of the Shang Dynasty!
You should employ virtuous people,
But you favor greed and tyranny.
You slander the virtuous with rumors,
Robbers and thieves surround you.
Praying to spirits to harm the loyal and good,
Your wicked deeds are countless."

King Wen once lamented thus:
"Alas, you King Zhou of the Shang Dynasty!
You're rampant and arrogant,

Treating the wicked as loyal subjects.
Good and evil are indistinguishable,
There are no wise men by your side.
Without discernment of right and wrong,
You have neither loyal ministers nor courtiers."

King Wen once lamented thus:
"Alas, you King Zhou of the Shang Dynasty!
Heaven does not allow you to indulge in drinking,
You should not engage in unjust acts.
Your behavior and demeanor are gravely flawed,
You lack self-control day and night.
Drunkenly shouting and disorderly,
Treating night as day."

King Wen once lamented thus:
"Alas, you King Zhou of the Shang Dynasty!
The political landscape is in disarray like cicada songs,
Boiling over like bubbling soup.
Major and minor affairs all end in ruin,
You pursue a single-minded path.
The anger of the people at home grows,
Their fury extends in all directions."

King Wen once lamented thus:
"Alas, you King Zhou of the Shang Dynasty!
It is not that Heaven is unkind,
It is you who have abandoned the old laws.
Though you may lack elder ministers,
There are ancestral traditions.
These principles you do not heed,
The fate of the nation will decline."

King Wen once lamented thus:
"Alas, you King Zhou of the Shang Dynasty!
People often say these words:
'Toppling a great tree starts with its roots,

Though its branches and leaves remain undamaged,
Its foundation has been uprooted.
The lessons of the Shang Dynasty are not distant,
The fate of King Jie of the Xia Dynasty is before our eyes.'"

RESTRAINT (抑)

A person of virtuous appearance and humble demeanor,
Their moral character must be upright.
People often say an old saying:
"Great wisdom appears as foolishness."
The ignorance of common people,
That is a common fault.
The wise appear foolish in their eyes,
This is an unusual circumstance.

To prosper as a nation, we need virtuous people,
Then the lords of the four directions will obey.
With upright moral conduct,
The lords of the four directions will submit.
Grand plans should be well-defined,
Far-reaching strategies made clear.
Conduct should be cautious and prudent,
The people should take this as a model.

Now, observe the current situation,
The state's politics are chaotic, and no one listens.
From top to bottom, moral character is corrupted,
Indulging in drunken revelry.
They only know how to indulge in drink and pleasure,
The great achievements of their ancestors are hard to inherit.
The kings of old did not seek expansion,
How can the laws of wisdom and brightness be followed?

Heaven will not bless us again,
As if a spring had run dry.

One after another, disasters will strike,
We should rise early and sleep late,
Just as a hall should be regularly swept.
You, as a leader, should set the example.
Repair your chariots and horses,
Ensure that bows and arrows are ready.
Be vigilant; war could erupt at any time,
Conquer the tribes of the barbarians.

Treat your subjects with care,
Abide by the laws of lords and princes.
Be cautious of unforeseen accidents.
Speak with caution,
Let your words and actions be proper,
Always be kind and have a pleasant countenance.
If white jade has blemishes,
They can be polished away cleanly.
But if words are spoken incorrectly,
They cannot be retrieved.

Do not easily express your opinions,
Words should not be spoken carelessly.
Though no one restrains your tongue,
Once words are spoken, they cannot be changed.
There is no speech without a response,
No kindness without reward for good deeds.
Be friendly to colleagues and superiors,
Do not look down on common people.
Descendants and future generations are countless,
All the people will be obedient.

Treat colleagues and superiors kindly,
With a gentle and amiable countenance.
Avoid causing others to dislike you.
When you are alone in a dark room,
You should have a clear conscience and righteous
conduct.

Do not think that because the room is dark,
Your actions and beauty cannot be seen.
The spirits can come at any time,
Without notice and without prior sight,
Attempting to guess their arrival is futile.

Display your excellent moral character,
Act with virtue in all your endeavors.
Be cautious in your actions and exhibit a pleasing countenance.
Let your conduct be without fault and never regretful.
Do not commit wrongdoing or harm others,
Become an exemplary figure with a good reputation.
If you offer me a peach,
I will repay you with a sweet plum.
Mischievous and foolish children,
Their minds are confused and lack reason.

The zither wood, paulownia, and lacquer are both soft and hard,
Crafted into musical instruments with silk strings.
The elder with gentleness and humility,
Their moral foundation is praised by people.
Only the wise and virtuous can tell you,
Ancient words of wisdom to follow.
Abide by moral principles,
But these ignorant and muddled people,
Might say that my words are hollow,
As hearts and minds vary and are hard to discern.

The young and inexperienced are still very young,
They cannot distinguish between good and bad!
Not only do I have to teach you,
But I have also advised you on your affairs.
Face to face, I explained carefully,
Pulling your ears to make you listen.
Young and ignorant, you might still be forgiven,

But now you have children in your arms.
People should be humble and not self-satisfied,
Who can be wise early or late in life?

Heaven sees everything clearly,
My life has not been happy.
Seeing you act clueless,
My heart is distressed and sorrowful.
Honestly and earnestly, I taught you,
But you disregarded my words.
You don't need my guidance,
Instead, you use my words as jokes.
You say you are still young and inexperienced,
But in reality, you are no longer a child!

Young and inexperienced, do not be arrogant,
Listen to the ancient laws and regulations.
If you follow my advice,
You will not regret and face disaster.
The world's situation is difficult now,
The nation may be on the verge of ruin.
This example is not far off,
Heaven's retribution is imminent.
If your perverse nature remains unchanged,
It will bring great calamity to the people!

GENTLE MULBERRIES (桑柔)

Lush mulberry trees with tender branches,
Beneath them, a pleasant shade of green.
But when the leaves are all plucked,
The destitute people have no shelter.
Endless worries fill my heart,
Sorrow and grief have left me desolate.
The incomparably bright heavens above,
Seemingly show no mercy upon me.

Four strong horses continue to gallop,
Colorful banners fluttering in the wind.
Disasters and chaos erupt without end,
No nation remains unscathed.
The young and strong among the people perish,
All suffering perils and death.
Alas, I sigh with a heavy heart,
The nation is in dire straits, causing great pain.

The country is in chaos, wealth depleted,
Heaven no longer supports the Zhou dynasty.
Nowhere to find a place of refuge,
Unsure of where to turn.
Gentlemen, think deeply,
In your hearts, prioritize the nation.
Who created this disaster?
To this day, we still face calamity.

Sorrow and anguish weigh heavily on my heart,
Longing for my hometown and ancestral land.
Born in troubled times, it's truly lamentable,

Caught in Heaven's wrath and fury.
People fleeing from west to east,
No place to find respite.
Encountering hardships in abundance,
The borders are in distress, what can we do?

Strategize carefully to reduce the chaos,
With your best efforts, worry for the nation.
Encourage the wise and capable,
Who can endure the intense summer heat
And not seek relief in the cool waters?
If the state of affairs does not improve,
One after another, we all shall perish.

It's like struggling against a strong wind,
Breathing becomes difficult.
People have a desire to achieve,
But not everyone's strengths can be utilized.
Agriculture should be highly regarded,
Officials working hard to provide grain.
Agricultural production is a treasure,
With ample grain, the country prospers.

Disasters and deaths are descending from Heaven,
Seeking to annihilate our kings.
Countless pests are unleashed,
Devouring crops and grains.
It is truly lamentable, my China,
Famine and calamity are relentless.
We are already exhausted,
Only able to appeal to the heavens.

Only a wise and virtuous king,
Is revered by the people.
With a bright and just rule,
Carefully selecting wise ministers.
Only the unrighteous and foolish king,

Revels in his own enjoyment.
With a heart full of wickedness,
He confuses and drives the people to madness.

Look at those dense forests,
Numerous wild deer gather in herds.
Yet among friends, deception abounds,
Lack of goodwill prevents them from drawing near.
People often say such things:
"To advance or retreat, both are miserable."

Only the sage has far-sightedness,
Seeing clearly beyond a hundred miles.
Only the fool is utterly foolish,
Pleased by immediate gains and losses.
It is not that they cannot speak,
Why are they so fearful?

For those with good intentions,
They do not seek extravagant gains,
But for those who are ruthless and cruel,
They do not loosen their grip on power.
People fear that heaven will become chaotic,
And would rather endure torment than perish.

The violent wind surely has its way,
In the open valleys, it finds its source.
For those with good intentions,
They walk the path of virtue and are praised.
For those who do not understand the principles,
They sink into a muddy pit.

The violent wind surely has its way,
Greed and corruption harm the virtuous.
When advice is given and met with agreement,
When counsel is heard, they pretend to be intoxicated.
Honorable advice and good words are ignored,

Instead, they claim my reasoning is flawed.

My colleagues and friends,
Do I not know your intentions?
Like little birds flying erratically,
Sometimes shot down from the sky.
I came to offer sincere advice to help you,
But you responded with intimidation and defiance.

The people's behavior lacks direction,
Because officials deceive them.
They specialize in harming the people,
Not harming the hearts of the good.
The people's conduct is not upright,
Because the government imposes oppressive policies.

The people still live in distress,
Because bandits and thieves roam free.
I earnestly advise against this path,
Behind your back, I sing a song for you to hear.

HEAVENLY DROUGHT (云汉)

The vast and boundless Milky Way,
Ceaselessly turns in the sky.
King Zhou looks up and sighs,
"What sins have the people committed?
Heaven sends continuous calamities,
Famine and disasters follow one another.
Offerings to every deity are made,
Sacrifices of all kinds are given.
But the sacred jade and precious discs are exhausted,
My prayers go unanswered."

The severe drought is indeed relentless,
The scorching heat feels like steaming.
Sacrifices have never ceased,
From suburban rituals to ancestral temples.
All the gods of heaven and earth are revered,
Every deity is treated with utmost respect.
Have our ancestors and Houji forsaken us?
Has God ceased to grace us?
The people on the earth suffer immensely,
Why has this calamity befallen us?

The severe drought is indeed relentless,
The situation cannot be alleviated.
We are filled with fear and unease,
As if thunder is about to strike.
The remaining people of the Zhou dynasty,
Have no hope of survival.
The boundless and vast God above,
Seems to have no sympathy for us.

Why can't love and benevolence be bestowed?
Even relying on our ancestors seems in vain.

The severe drought is indeed relentless,
Attempts to stop it prove futile.
The sun blazes like fire, scorching,
Nowhere to escape the heat's grip.
Our lifespans are about to end,
Heaven turns a blind eye.
The spirits of the ancient and righteous,
Do not come to our aid in this adversity.
Even our parents and ancestors,
How can they bear to not save us?

The severe drought is indeed relentless,
Rivers and streams have dried, vegetation withered.
The drought deity's malevolence knows no bounds,
The scorching sun burns fiercely.
In our hearts, we fear the scorching heat,
Worry and agony like an ordeal.
The spirits of the ancient and righteous,
Do they not hear my cries?
The God above the vast heavens,
Where can I flee to?

The severe drought is indeed relentless,
Though we pray with all our hearts, we're still anxious.
Why does this cruel drought torment us?
The reasons behind it remain unknown.
Praying for the Year and offering sacrifices is not too
late,
The Fangshe ritual comes early.
The God above the vast heavens,
Why does He not aid and show mercy?
We have shown utmost respect to the deities,
Surely they should not be offended.

The severe drought is indeed relentless,
Officials cannot afford to be distracted.
Government officials fall into poverty,
Even high-ranking ministers suffer illness.
The officials who tend to the horses and those who educate,
Cooks and close advisers to the king,
King Zhou provides relief to all,
Aiding the people without pause.
Gazing up at the vast heavenly realm,
When will this sorrow end?

Gazing up at the boundless heavenly realm,
Countless stars brightly twinkle.
Esteemed officials and high-ranking officers,
Pray to the gods without pause or delay.
Our lifespans are coming to an end,
Do not abandon our previous efforts, do not fear hardship.
Praying for rain is not just for ourselves,
But also for the stability of high-ranking officers.
Look up and gaze at the expansive heavens,
When will my heart find peace?

SUBLIME SONG (嵩高)

Majestic and towering, Mount Taiyue stands,
Soaring high to reach the heavens above.
It's here that Taiyue bestows its blessings,
Giving birth to two virtuous souls, Shenfu.
Shenbo and Shenfu, noble and wise,
They are the pillars of the Zhou dynasty.
Relying on them as protective shields,
The king's grace they wholeheartedly proclaim.

Diligent and tireless, Shenbo labors,
Assisting the Zhou king in preserving ancestral heritage.
He constructs cities and fortresses,
A role model for the southern lords.
The king commands his ministers to summon Shenbo,
To secure his dwelling in the south.
Thus, a southern state is built,
To be safeguarded for generations unchanged.

The Zhou king commands Shenbo,
To be an exemplar in the southern realm.
Depending on the people of Xie's domain,
Build sturdy walls for protection.
The Zhou king instructs Shenbo,
To manage his territorial fields.
And the court appoints attendants,
To accompany his journey forward.

Shenbo's construction brings great achievement,
And Shenfu continues the endeavor.
Perfect and resilient renovations,

Temples, ancestral shrines, all constructed.
The new temple and shrine are truly magnificent,
The king rewards Shenbo's great deeds:
Four strong steeds, mighty and robust,
Adorned with gleaming treasures.

The king bids Shenbo to Xie's city,
Sending him off with a retinue.
"I have carefully considered your abode,
The south is the more suitable place.
I bestow upon you this precious jade disc,
As a treasure to safeguard the state.
Go quickly, O King's Uncle,
Guard the land of the south."

Shenbo decides to embark on his journey,
The king bids him farewell in Mei.
Shenbo decides to return to the south,
With a sincere heart, he goes to Xie's city.
The Zhou king commands Duke Mu,
To delineate Shenbo's territorial boundaries.
Prepare an ample supply of provisions,
To hasten Shenbo's departure.

Shenbo, noble and valiant, marches forth,
Entering the newly constructed Xie's city.
His retinue, horses, all move with tranquility.
The people of Zhou rejoice with joyful expressions,
For their country possesses such a pillar.
This illustrious Shenbo,
Is the king's elder maternal uncle,
Renowned for his wisdom and valor.

Shenbo, praised by all for his virtuous character,
Gentle, honest, and of a kind disposition.
He pacifies the various vassal states,
His good name spreads to all corners.

Jifu composed this song,
A heartfelt tribute with verses long.
Its beautiful melody is sung with affection,
To convey the depths of feelings for Shenbo.

THE PEOPLE'S WELFARE (烝民)

Heaven gave birth to the multitude of people,
In this world, all things have their norms.
The people's nature follows this logic,
Naturally inclined towards good conduct.
Heaven observes the Zhou dynasty,
With sincere prayers to the divine.
Bless the present Zhou sovereign,
Granting the birth of Shang Fu for peace.

Shang Fu possesses noble character,
Gentle, kind, and principled.
His demeanor is warm and pleasing,
His actions meticulous and outstanding.
He adheres to the ancient teachings,
Conduct and etiquette align perfectly.
In obedience to the king's will,
The king appoints him to decree policies.

King Zhou commands Zhong Shang Fu:
To be an exemplar for the feudal lords,
Inheriting the accomplishments of ancestors,
Protecting the king's well-being.
At all times, convey the king's commands,
You shall be the king's voice.
Disseminate royal decrees beyond the capital,
Implement them thoroughly throughout the realm.

The king's decrees are solemn and sacred,
Shang Fu takes his mission seriously.
Whether governance in the states is good or bad,

Shang Fu discerns it most clearly.
His knowledge is profound, his judgment keen,
Preserving his integrity brings renown.
He rises early and sleeps late without weariness,
Wholeheartedly serving the king with virtue.

Among the people, this saying prevails:
Pick ripe persimmons to savor,
Discard the ones too hard to bite.
But this Zhong Shang Fu,
He doesn't eat the soft ones,
Nor does he fear the hard ones.
He never oppresses widows and orphans,
Nor is he intimidated by bullies.

Common wisdom also holds:
Virtue is as light as a feather,
Yet people find it hard to lift.
However, Zhong Shang Fu,
With careful reflection and deep thought,
Loves to aid those in distress.
When the king's decrees have shortcomings,
Only Shang Fu can rectify them.

Shang Fu sets out to offer sacrifices to the road deities,
With four magnificent horses striding proudly.
His mounted soldiers move swiftly,
Lest they be late with hearts anxious.
Four splendid horses, truly majestic,
Eight phoenix bells resound melodiously.
The king issues commands to Shang Fu,
To build a new city in the east.

Four sturdy horses gallop swiftly,
Eight phoenix bells chime incessantly.
Shang Fu heads to Qi to build the city,
Upon completion, he swiftly returns to the capital.

Jifu composes a farewell song,
A melodious tune like a gentle breeze.
Shang Fu, away from home, longs for it,
Finding solace in this parting song.

HAN YI (韩奕)

Lofty and towering, the Liangshan stands high,
Great Yu controlled floods, waters no longer nigh.
A grand road wide and vast in its span,
Han Hou goes to court, receiving the king's plan.
King Zhou himself decreed and said with grace,
"Inherit our ancestors' deeds, take your place.
Never forsake my orders, heed them tight,
Rise early, rest late, with all your might.
Loyal in your duties, be cautious, I pray,
I won't lightly grant you your role today.
Stabilize unruly states that are far,
Assist the king, serve with your star."

Four strong horses, fat and robust,
Sturdy bodies, tall and finely robust.
Han Hou enters the capital with esteem,
In hand a great jade, to the court he'll redeem.
Prostrate at the altar, he greets King Zhou,
The king rewards him, gifts he bestows.
Embroidered dragon banners, feathers arrayed,
Bamboo curtains and painted carriages displayed.
Black dragon robe, red shoes that gleam,
Horses with Fan plumes, a golden gleam.
Mongolian fur, tiger hide beams,
Yoke and harness, golden gleams.

Homeward bound, Han Hou pays respects to road
deities,
Resting at Tu Cheng on the way with ease.
His father shows up to see him off,

A hundred pots of pure wine, fragrant enough.
What dishes did he prepare that day?
Steamed armorfish, delicious, they say.
For side dishes, vegetables were presented,
Fresh bamboo shoots and tender reed sprouts resented.
What gifts did he give Han Hou, pray?
Four-horse carriages, grand on display.
Wicker baskets, beans, and fruits arrayed,
Lords merrily drinking, feeling gay.

In this place, Han Hou takes a wife,
Li Wang's niece, to be his life.
She's the daughter of Duke Que's clan,
Han Hou marries her, a noble plan.
In Duke Que's city, a grand parade,
A hundred large carriages in serenade.
Eight phoenix bells resound with grace,
His status shines brightly, a glorious embrace.
Many concubines accompany the bride,
Each one beautiful, side by side.
Han Hou turns around to see,
His bride and concubines, all lovely to be.

Duke Que is powerful, skilled in war's art,
Conquering various lands, from the start.
Seeking a husband for his daughter's hand,
No place like Han, the most fertile land.
Living here is joyful, nothing to bemoan,
Rivers and wetlands, vast and grown.
Fish in the waters leap and frolic,
Doe and stag, in the mountains frolic.
Deep forests, bears and tigers stalk,
Leopards roam, wild in their walk.
A splendid dwelling, now they reside,
Han Hou and Han Jie, their joy does not hide.

The vast and spectacular city of Han,

Built by the people since the clan began.
Since ancestors received their decree,
Relied on these Bai Man, gradually they grew free.
King Zhou, for his merits, rewards Han Hou's sway,
The Mo and Ma tribes under his ray.
Northern states, all in his hand,
As Lord Fang Bo, he manages the land.
Builds cities, digs moats, waters flow,
Tills the land, turns the soil below.
Chases the Mo, they offer their trade,
Red leopard and yellow tiger skins laid.

JIANG HAN (江汉)

The Yangtze and Han rivers surge and swell,
Warriors march forth with a battle cry's swell.
Not for pleasure or leisure they roam,
But to quell the rebellion in Huai's home.
War chariots roll and banners rise high,
Not for comfort or frolic, but to imply,
They'll halt the invasion of Huai's clan,
Protecting the kingdom from their malevolent plan.

The Yangtze and Han rivers flow so wide,
Warriors march with valor, side by side.
Conquering rebellious lands, they strive,
To report success, to please the king alive.
Rebels defeated, peace to the land,
The kingdom stabilized, with a steady hand.
Now, as war ceases and calmness begins,
The king finds solace within.

By the banks of the Yangtze and Han's flow,
The king summoned Tiger to bestow,
A task to expand the kingdom's domain,
To govern our borders, the land to maintain.
Be gentle with the people, patience you'll need,
The kingdom's welfare, it's your creed.
Settle the boundaries, sow fields anew,
To the southern seas, distant and true.

The king commanded Duke Tiger so,
To enforce his decrees, wherever they go.
"Inherited by fate, both talent and name,

My ancestors esteemed you, with no shame.
Don't say that I am still so young,
The legacy is yours; it must be sung.
Strive for success, seek to excel,
May the gods grant you fortune and dwell."

Duke Tiger humbly bowed, full of grace,
Thanking the king for his embrace,
For a square bronze vessel, specially made,
Wishing the king endless years, it conveyed.
The king, diligent and clear in his reign,
His noble reputation, it would sustain.
Civilized and virtuous, his rule well-founded,
Nations prospered, peace resounded.

CHANGWU (常武)

Glorious and wise, King Xuan of Zhou,
Ordered his officials to the South pursue.
In the ancestral temple, he decreed the call,
Nan Zhong, Grand Master Huang Fu, should heed it all.
Organize the mighty six armies at your command,
Prepare war chariots, arrows, bows in hand.
Stay vigilant and ever cautious, take care,
Show benevolence to the people everywhere.

The king commanded the Yin family's might,
With Lord Cheng Bo leading the fight.
The entire army in formations aligned,
Soldiers were warned; their departure assigned.
Along the banks of the Huai River, they'd roam,
Inspect Xu's territory, make it their home.
No lingering, no protracted stay,
All was prepared for the return way.

Glorious and resolute, King Xuan declared,
His anger's thunder, mightily flared.
Ordered the grand army to march ahead,
Their roars like tigers, they swiftly spread.
On high ground by the Huai, they'd deploy,
Countless prisoners they'd capture and enjoy.
Cutting off Huai's escape by river's flow,
In this battleground, they'd encamp and grow.

King Xuan's strategic mind was profound,
Xu State submitted; peace was soon found.
The land of Xu now belonged to Zhou's reign,

And for this great victory, they'd proclaim.
From all corners, rebellions were quelled,
The kingdom now firmly and stably held.
With war now ended and peace restored,
The king's heart in tranquility soared.

By the Yangtze and the Han's embrace,
King Xuan summoned Tiger to his grace:
"Expand the borders, take your quest,
Consolidate our realm, be our best.
Handle the people with a gentle hand,
The kingdom's welfare is what I command.
Define the boundaries, cultivate the land,
To the southern sea, we make our stand."

The king decreed to the Yin family's might,
Cheng Bo was appointed to oversee the right.
The entire army in formation stood tall,
They were told to heed the king's call.
Marching along the Huai River's side,
Inspecting Xu's lands far and wide.
No time for lingering or delay,
Prepared for their return on this day.

Glorious and resolute, King Xuan's decree,
His anger's thunder, mighty as the sea.
The grand army marched forth in might,
Their battle cries fierce, their spirits bright.
On high ground by the Huai, they'd deploy,
Countless prisoners they'd capture and enjoy.
Cutting off Huai's escape, firm and strong,
In this battleground, they'd right the wrong.

King Xuan's wisdom, a guiding light,
With Xu State's submission, peace took flight.
The land of Xu now belonged to Zhou's reign,
And for this great victory, they'd proclaim.

Rebellions quelled from every side,
The kingdom was stable, in peace it would bide.
With war now ended and peace restored,
The king's heart in tranquility soared.

ZHAN YANG (瞻卬)

Gazing up at the vast and distant sky,
Heaven refuses to bestow blessings from high.
The world, for ages, knows no peace,
Enduring catastrophes and troubles that cease.
In times of turmoil and instability,
The people suffer immensely, it's plain to see.
Thieves and villains plague every land,
Suffering and hardships, hand in hand.
Criminals roam freely, without a hitch,
Leaving the people in a state of unease, which is rich.

Taking land from others, a ruthless gain,
Stealing servants and causing pain.
Innocents, wrongly accused and confined,
Their freedom stripped, no justice they find.
Those truly guilty should be justly tried,
But you let them go free, casting justice aside.
The wise build cities, it's their call,
But some women scheme, causing the fall.
Spreading rumors, creating strife and hate,
Their ability to do harm is truly innate.
Calamity doesn't fall from the sky above,
Evil emerges from the hearts of women, and love
Is blind when it comes to palace eunuchs' lies,
The king heeds them, to everyone's surprise.

Accusations and schemes, they never cease,
Contradictory words, confusion increase.
Can we say wickedness has no bounds?
Can we deny that evil abounds?

Merchants seek profit in trade,
Statesmen govern, decisions they've made.
Women, stay out of state affairs, it's plain,
For weaving and silk, your skills should remain.

Why has heaven punished us so?
Why no blessings from high, do we show?
Discarding the villain, the source of our pain,
We heed ill advice, suspicion we gain.
No sympathy for the disasters we bear,
No proper decorum, it's all too clear.
Wise men and loyal subjects all fled,
Leaving the nation in turmoil and dread.

Heaven's calamity strikes far and wide,
Suffering people from every side.
Wise men departed, away they sped,
Their hearts heavy with worries left unsaid.
Heaven's calamity now engulfs us all,
The nation in peril, citizens stand tall.
Wise men departed, no solace found,
Their sorrow and grief, there's no respite around.

Fountains once burst with splendor and grace,
Now they've run dry, a deserted place.
A deep, clear pool once so profound,
Now is parched, nowhere's water found.
Calamity has swept across the land,
Its devastation vast, hard to withstand.
Should we not fear heaven's grand design?
Respect our ancestors, for our children's line.

SHAO MIN (召旻)

Heaven acts violently and irrationally,
Sending down immense calamities, so tragically.
Suffering from hunger and pain so dire,
The people flee, seeking to retire.
Their abodes lie desolate and forlorn.

Heaven casts a wide net in its decree,
Rebellion and infighting, chaos to decree.
Mutual slander and disrespect,
Debauchery and ignorance unchecked,
How can this person befit Zhou?

Endless plots and schemes are rife,
Unbeknownst, they harbor their own strife.
The nobleman's diligence and dedication,
No rest, no leisure, no hesitation,
Positions repeatedly revoked and deposed.

Now it's like a vast drought's blight,
The land's wild grasses withered from sight,
Like dry grasses toppled in a row,
Upon observing the state, despair begins to grow.

Once prosperous, now impoverished we stand,
The hardship today at its peak, understand.
Trading vegetables for rice in our despair,
Why not return home and take proper care?
The turmoil worsens with each passing day.

The water in the pond slowly dries,

No more flowing, the source now lies.
The fountain's water gradually ebbs away,
Its springhead now severed, as they say,
Calamity spreads throughout our nation,
And yet, you're unafraid of your own foundation.

In times of yore, Heaven granted the mandate,
Numerous wise advisors as allies so great.
Each day, a hundred miles newly acquired,
But now, each day, a hundred miles retired,
Leaving hearts sorrowful and full of pain.
Look at the current leaders, what's their gain?

ODES (颂)

The "Mao Shi Xu" states, "Odes describe the beautiful and virtuous, announcing their success to the deities." This indicates that they are songs of worship for ancestral temples. The poems in the "Odes" are not only meant to be played but can also be sung and danced, used for performances. They have a slow tempo, some are unrhymed, and they are not divided into chapters.

Zhou Odes

There are thirty-one poems in the "Zhou Odes," which are hymns from the Zhou Dynasty primarily used for ancestral temple worship. All of them were composed during the Western Zhou period, originating in the capital city of the Western Zhou, Haojing.

CLEAR TEMPLE (清廟)

In the Clear and Serene Temple so beautiful,
Assisting in the noble and dignified rites.
Scholars gather in orderly lines to perform the sacrifice,
The virtues of King Wen are deeply remembered.
Gazing afar at King Wen in the heavenly realm,
In the temple, ceaseless movements and steps.
His radiance shines, passed down through the ages,
Admiration for him knows no bounds.

THE MANDATE OF HEAVEN (维天之命)

Contemplate the workings of the celestial way,
Beautiful and solemn, unceasing.
How splendid and bright it is,
The virtue of King Wen, so pure!
Such virtuous excellence makes me cautious,
We must forever uphold it.
Following the path of our ancestor, King Wen,
Generation after generation shall carry it out.

CLEAR (维清)

Our Zhou governance is clear and bright,
The regulations of King Wen serve as a guiding light.
Great achievements began in the Western Land,
Ultimately, our foundation is established.
This is the auspicious sign of the Zhou lineage.

ILLUSTRIOUS VIRTUE (烈文)

For your merits and virtues, numerous lords,
Heaven bestows upon you immense blessings.
Your grace and favor are immeasurable,
May your descendants long enjoy this good fortune.
Do not let great mistakes befall your state,
Devote your heart to honoring the Zhou sovereign.
Remember your ancestors' great deeds,
Continue to achieve greatness and propagate it.
A nation's strength lies in having talented individuals,
From all directions, they will come to submit.
Our ancestors were great in virtue,
You, gentlemen, should serve as exemplars.
Ah, the exemplary model of our forefathers, never to be
forgotten!

HEAVEN'S DECREE (天作)

Heaven above has created Mount Qi so high,
King Tai cultivated the land, clearing it of weeds.
The people here built new houses,
King Wen allowed the people to enjoy peace and well-being.
The people rush to the vicinity of Mount Qi,
The road to Mount Qi is wide and open.
May the descendants forever protect this place.

THE MANDATE FROM GRAND HEAVEN (昊天有成命)

Clearly, Grand Heaven has given its command,
King Wen and King Wu received the mandate.
King Cheng did not dare to enjoy peace and well-being,
Day and night, he secured the people and followed Heaven's decree.
Ah, how radiant and splendid it is!
Striving with all one's might to fulfill Heaven's mandate,
The nation enjoys peace and the people are at ease.

MY OFFERING (我将)

I offer sacrifices to the divine,
With cattle and sheep as the offering,
Praying for Heaven's blessings upon Zhou.
Following the regulations of King Wen,
Daily seeking peace in all directions.
The great King Wen's name resounds,
Fit to be offered to the Supreme Deity.
Morning and evening, we labor diligently,
In awe of Heaven's will,
To ensure the prosperity of our Zhou.

MARCHING FORTH (时迈)

King Wu visited the various states,
Heaven regarded him as its son.
Blessing our mighty Zhou with prosperity,
He led our troops to defeat King Zhou,
All four corners of the world were in awe.
Appeasing the myriad spirits through sacrifice,
Mountains, rivers, and countless spirits joined in.
King Wu, the ruler of all nations!
Unparalleled glory for the great Zhou,
Rewarding in order of merit.
Laying down our weapons and armor,
Storing bows and sharp arrows in our bags.
Emphasizing virtuous conduct,
Extending it throughout the land.
May the Zhou reign forever prosper!

COMPETENCE (执竞)

King Wu conquered the Shang with his might,
No one could surpass his martial achievements.
Kings Cheng and Kang, wise rulers,
Even the Deity praised them.
Under King Cheng and King Kang's rule,
Zhou unified all four corners,
Clear governance and education in the court.
The bells and drums resound,
The chimes and musical pipes ring,
Heaven sends abundant blessings.
Spirits descend with great auspiciousness,
The ceremonies are grand and meticulous.
The spirits are sated and inebriated,
Blessings and wealth continuously bestowed upon Zhou.

SOVEREIGN OF VIRTUE (思文)

King Houji, unsurpassed in virtue,
His merits can be compared to the heavens.
Stabilizing the world and its people,
No one remained unrewarded by his grace.
He bestowed upon us the gift of wheat,
Imperial decree to use it for sustenance.
Without distinction or borders,
Spread throughout all of China.

DUTIFUL OFFICIALS (臣工)

Ministers and officials, hear me out,
Handle state affairs with caution.
The king rewards your merits,
He is here to comfort and inquire.
Agricultural officials, heed the command,
It is now late spring,
What requests do you have? Speak up,
How are the new and old fields to be cultivated?
Barley and wheat are growing well,
Autumn will bring a good harvest.
The most radiant Deity,
Bestows upon us a bountiful year.
Command the farmers:
Prepare your hoes and other tools,
Witness the scene of the harvest.

YI HEI (噫嘻)

Yi Hei, may King Cheng bless us,
With utmost sincerity, we reach out to the heavens.
Leading the farmers to the fields,
Various crops are quickly sown.
Hurry, pick up your farming tools,
Plow the fields diligently before you.
Your cultivation must be meticulous,
Thousands of people labor together.

RISING HERON (振鹭)

White heron spreading its wings, soaring in the sky,
Landing in the vast western marshes.
I have a guest who has come to visit,
Adorned in noble white attire.
In his feudal state, no one bears grievances,
Here, he is admired by all.
May he govern diligently and wisely,
Forever spreading his good name far and wide.

BOUNTIFUL YEAR (丰年)

In a bountiful year, millet and rice are abundant,
Granaries tall and full.
Storing billions of new grains,
Brewing sweet and fragrant wine,
Offering it to our ancestors to taste.
In harmony with the ceremony,
Abundant blessings and great auspiciousness descend.

THE BLIND MUSICIAN (有瞽)

Blind musicians in rows they stand,
Gathering in the courtyard before the Zhou Temple.
Drum stands and bell stands arranged,
Adorned with colorful feathers.
Both small and large drums are there,
Bronze and stone chimes in perfect order.
All musical instruments ready to play,
Flutes and pipes resound together.
The music fills the ears, truly melodious,
Solemn and harmonious, a soothing sound,
Ancestors and spirits come to appreciate.
All guests have assembled,
Applause follows the performance in unison.

HIDDEN (潜)

Ah, the beautiful Qi River and Ju River,
Abode of various fishes.
Including lampreys and sturgeons,
And also mudfish and grass carp.
Offered in sacrifice to our ancestors,
Seeking boundless blessings and fortune.

PIOUS (雝)

Arriving calmly and composed,
Entering the temple with reverence.
Assisting in the sacrifice are nobles and lords,
The main celebrant, the Son of Heaven, sincere and respectful.
Presenting a large sacrificial ox,
Helping to arrange the offerings for the divine.
Great and radiant Father King,
Comforting the hearts of filial sons.
Each minister understands the principles,
The king excels in both civil and martial arts.
God is peaceful and joyful,
Blessing the prosperity of descendants.
Praying for longevity,
Blessings, and abundant happiness.
Urging the Father King to partake,
Inviting the Queen Mother to taste.

AUDIENCE (载见)

The nobles visit King Zhou for the first time,
Requesting the new rituals.
Dragon and phoenix banners fluttering in the wind,
Chariots adorned with jingling bells.
Horse bridles gleaming with bronze ornaments,
Beautiful decorations sparkling brightly.
Respectfully paying homage to the ancestral spirits,
Honoring the offerings to the gods.
Praying to the divine for longevity,
Securing eternal peace and well-being,
Bestowing endless happiness.
Nobles are virtuous and capable,
The ancient kings bestow great blessings,
Enabling your endeavors to shine forever.

HONORED GUEST (有客)

Visitors from afar come to visit,
Driving white horses, strong and robust.
Accompanied by numerous attendants,
All of them possess virtuous character.
The guests have stayed for two days,
A longer stay is welcomed.
Providing them with horse tether ropes,
Restraining the horses from moving.
Farewelling the guests from a distance,
Ministers on both sides are warm-hearted.
Using great virtue to treat the guests,
Bringing down abundant blessings.

MARTIAL (武)

Ah, our great King Wu,
Unparalleled in grand achievements.
Following the virtuous path of King Wen,
Laying the foundation for the Zhou.
King Wu inherited his legacy,
Defeating King Zhou and ending his tyranny,
Ultimately achieving magnificent feats.

A YOUNG SON (闵予小子)

Pity the young son who ascends the throne,
His family faces misfortune at home.
Lonely, sad, and grieving,
Ah, my father, King Wu, so wise,
Throughout his life, he honored our ancestors.
Thinking of my great grandfather,
Ruling with righteousness and following the Way.
Though I am a young child,
I must diligently govern day and night.
Ah, great ancestors and kings,
I will forever uphold your legacy and not forget.

INQUIRIES (访落)

I have just ascended to the throne, needing advice,
Emulating the unwavering aspirations of the ancient kings.
Sighing with concerns in my heart,
Youthful and lacking experience.
Ministers support me, following the law,
Continuing the ancestral legacy, unwavering.
I am a young and inexperienced child,
Facing many hardships and unable to bear them.
Inheriting the path of governance from my forefathers,
Appointing ministers in order of precedence.
My father, the wise and great King,
Bless me with everlasting prosperity.

RESPECTFUL (敬之)

Beware, oh beware,
Heaven observes with keen eyes, not to be deceived.
Earning Heaven's mandate is not easy.
Don't say Heaven is distant and high,
Actions below are swift and speedy,
Heaven watches over both you and me.
I, a young and inexperienced child,
Should be wise and cautious.
Achieving something every day, progressing every month,
Learning and accumulating, gradually becoming clear.
Bearing significant responsibilities,
Remembering virtuous deeds.

MINOR ODES (小毖)

I remember past mistakes to prevent future harm,
No one else invited the stinging bees,
It was my own doing that brought trouble.
Now I believe, the little oriole,
Grows up to become a large bird.
I, who cannot endure the difficulties of the state,
Am now plunged into such bitterness.

CLEARING (載芟)

Pulling out weeds and removing tree roots,
The field has been plowed, the soil fresh.
A thousand people working shoulder to shoulder,
New fields extending to the old ones.
Elders lead their eldest sons,
Uncles and younger relatives also join.
Strong men and laborers all work diligently.
The sounds of eating in the wild are loud,
Husbands praise the delicious meal,
Wives love their husbands as their support.
The plowshare is sharp as a knife,
Cultivating the field under the sun's rays.
Various grains are sown into the soil,
Every seed full of vitality.
Seedlings continuously break through the soil,
Strong seedlings emerge first.
The rice seedlings are neat and lush,
The rice grains form dense heads.
During the harvest season, people are bustling,
Granaries and warehouses overflowing,
Countless grains impossible to calculate.
Clear wine and sweet wine in barrels,
Abundant harvest, offering to ancestors,
All rituals harmonious and perfect.
Delicious dishes spread fragrant aromas,
The nation is thriving.
The intoxicating aroma fills the house,
Elders are at peace, in high spirits.
This event is not unique to this place,
Not just this year celebrating the abundant harvest,

It has been this way from ancient times.

DILIGENT FARMER (良耜)

Sharp plowshare pierces the earth,
Beginning to till the field under the sun.
In spring, sowing a hundred grains,
Every seed bursting with vitality.
People come to watch in the field,
Carrying baskets of packed lunches,
Inside, millet rice is stored.
Wearing woven round straw hats,
They pick up hoes and weed,
Thistles and weeds all removed.
Thistles and weeds decay into fertilizers,
Crops grow luxuriant and strong.
The sound of reaping is bustling,
Crops are gathered, the field full.
Grain piles high like city walls,
Neat and orderly like the teeth of a comb.
Opening every family's grain barn,
The barns are full to the brim,
Women and children are content.
A large bull is slaughtered,
Its horns curving long and elegant.
Rituals have been performed year after year,
The ancestral traditions continue.

SILK CLOTHING (丝衣)

Silk garments for the sacrificial ceremony, white and pure,
Wearing leather hats, dignified and proper.
From the temple hall to the doorsteps,
Both sheep and cattle are abundant.
Large and small cauldrons are filled with food,
Curved wine cups all arranged,
The taste of the fine wine is pure.
Speeches are gentle, without arrogance,
Everyone lives long, practicing kindness.

LIBATIONS (酌)

Ah, the valiant and mighty king's army,
Wielding their forces, they conquered the Shang.
The Zhou's way shines brightly, the situation is good,
Hence, there were loyal warriors assisting King Zhou.
Lucky to receive the favor of Heaven,
Brave warriors pledged themselves to King Wu.
King Wu used them to conquer the Shang,
For the nation, he achieved fame and renown.

PROSPERITY (桓)

Stabilizing the states and territories under Heaven,
Years of abundant harvests, a favorable scene,
Heaven does not cease to favor the Zhou realm.
Mighty and glorious is King Wu,
Preserving the original homeland,
Dominating all four corners of the world,
Genuinely securing the Zhou state.
Magnificent deeds shine towards Heaven,
Replacing King Zhou as the sovereign.

BESTOWALS (赉)

King Wen's efforts were diligent,
I shall continue his path of governance.
Expanding the foundation endlessly,
I go to conquer the Shang for stability.
The Zhou state inherits Heaven's mandate,
Continuing the great legacy endlessly!

MINOR ODES (般)

Ah, the splendid brilliance of our Zhou state,
Ascending the towering mountains,
High peaks and small hills stretch endlessly,
A thousand branches and myriad streams flow into the
river.
Underneath the heavens, all the spirits gather,
Assembled here to enjoy the sacrifice,
Great Zhou receives the mandate for eternal longevity.

LU ODE (鲁颂)

Lu was the fief granted to Bo Qin, the eldest son of Duke Zhou, located in the area of present-day Qufu, Shandong. Because Duke Zhou had great achievements throughout the land, the ritual and music of the imperial court were granted to Bo Qin. This is how the "Lu Odes" originated, serving as songs for the temple. There are four poems in the "Lu Odes," all dating from the Spring and Autumn period. The place of origin is the capital of the state of Lu during the Spring and Autumn period, which is present-day Qufu, Shandong.

FINE HORSES (駉)

Majestic horses, strong and robust,
Grazing freely in the vast meadows.
Speaking of these vigorous horses,
Some have white tails, some gray coats,
Colors mixed, some chestnut, some yellow,
When harnessed to the chariots, they race ahead.
Running on the long and distant road,
These horses are sleek, well-fed, and strong.

Majestic horses, strong and robust,
Grazing freely in the vast meadows.
Speaking of these vigorous horses,
Some are dun-colored, some gray-dappled,
Some are bay with black manes, some are reddish-yellow,
When harnessed to war chariots, they charge into battle.
Majestic and powerful, their strength immeasurable,
These horses are sleek, well-fed, and strong.

Majestic horses, strong and robust,
Grazing freely in the vast meadows.
Speaking of these vigorous horses,
Some are blue with black backs, some are white,
Some are fiery red, and some are black as night,
When harnessed to chariots, they speed like the wind.
Endless energy, boundless in their abilities,
These horses are sleek, well-fed, and strong.

Majestic horses, strong and robust,
Grazing freely in the vast meadows.
Speaking of these vigorous horses,

Some are red and some have white markings,
Some are yellow-backed with white eyes like fish,
When pulling the carriages, their spirit soars.
Along the great road without deviation,
These horses race forward in haste.

VIGOROUS HORSES (有駜)

Vigorous and strong horses,
Four duns among them, all powerful.
Early to rise, late to rest, tending to official duties,
Diligent and hardworking for the state.
Holding egret feathers, they dance together,
Like white egrets soaring downward.
The drumbeat sounds incessantly,
Dancing tipsily after drinking.
Everyone is joyful and elated!

Vigorous and strong horses,
Four magnificent horses, full of spirit.
Early to rise, late to rest, tending to official duties,
Today, they drink in the public hall.
Holding egret feathers, they dance together,
Like white egrets soaring in the sky.
The drumbeat sounds incessantly,
Returning home after getting drunk, they stagger.
Everyone is joyful and elated!

Vigorous and strong horses,
Four green horses, full of vigor.
Early to rise, late to rest, tending to official duties,
Today, they celebrate in the public hall.
From now on, and forever,
Year after year, abundant harvests and auspicious scenes.
The ruler governs for the benefit of the people,
Leaving prosperity to descendants for a thousand years.
Everyone is joyful and elated!

WATERS OF PAN (泮水)

By the waters of Pan, everyone delights,
Some gather water celery by the banks.
The Duke of Lu comes in grand procession,
Already, the great banner with embroidered dragon
waves.
His dragon banner flutters in the wind,
Horse hooves create a melodious sound.
Officials, regardless of their rank,
All accompany the Duke to the gathering.

By the waters of Pan, everyone delights,
Some gather aquatic plants along the water's edge.
The Duke of Lu has arrived,
His carriage and horses are magnificent and tall.
His horses are high-spirited and robust,
His voice resounds powerfully.
His countenance is gentle, his smile warm,
He never gets angry, only teaches and guides.

By the waters of Pan, everyone delights,
Some gather water shield ferns by the water's edge.
The Duke of Lu has come here,
To this Pan Palace where the feast is set.
They enjoy fine wine, hearts elated,
Eternal spring of youth is bestowed.
Along the long and winding road,
Rebels are vanquished, calamities dispelled.

The Duke of Lu, with his dignified demeanor,
Cautiously cultivates his virtue.

His comportment is solemn and cautious,
A model for the people.
He possesses both literary and martial accomplishments,
His virtues can be compared to the ancients.
In everything, he emulates his ancestors,
Seeking endless blessings for himself.

The diligent and unrelenting Duke of Lu,
Cultivates his virtuous character with care.
The Pan Palace has been constructed,
The Huai tribes have surrendered in allegiance.
Brave generals like tigers,
Offering captives in celebration of success.
Judges inquire like Gao Tao,
The Pan Palace presents the fruits of victory.

In Lu, many wise individuals gather,
Magnifying the Duke of Lu's benevolent heart.
Mighty and brave, they march forth to subdue,
Cleansing the Di tribes along the southeast coast.
A grand army, their strength incomparable,
Silent and devoid of clamor,
Without fatigue, without disputes,
The Pan Palace offers the merits of vanquishing enemies.

The hornbows' strings are relaxed, bows not drawn,
Arrows lie stacked in bundles to the side.
War chariots are lined up in formation,
Foot soldiers no longer busy with their hands.
The Huai tribes have been conquered,
They bow down in obedience.
Resolutely following the Duke of Lu's strategies,
The Huai tribes ultimately surrender completely.

A graceful eagle owl soars in the sky,
Landing on the trees by Pan's banks.
Feasting on mulberries from our mulberry tree,

Repaying with melodious music in our ears.
The Huai tribes awaken to express remorse,
Specially coming to present their treasures.
Rare sightings of giant turtles and ivory,
Precious gems and southern gold, all offered.

BÌ PALACE (閟宮)

Bì Palace, solemn and pure,
Vast, profound, and rarely visited.
Lady Jiangyuan, illustrious and bright,
Her virtuous conduct shining pure and true.
The Heavenly Lord looked upon her,
With her, there were no calamities in childbirth.
She bore a child after ten months,
Jishe, intelligent from the start.
Heaven granted him a hundred blessings:
Millet and wheat ripening at different times,
Beans and barley planted at varied seasons.
Jishe taught farming to the world,
Planting tall millet and small millet,
As well as rice and dark millet, among others.
The four seas all belonged to Jishe,
Continuing the great work of Dayu.

Descendants of Jishe prospered greatly,
Taiwang being the most diligent.
He relocated to the southern slope of Qishan,
Preparing to overthrow the Yin and Shang.
The message reached King Wen and King Wu,
Inheriting Taiwang's aspirations.
Following the will of Heaven, they punished the guilty,
Swearing an oath on the battlefield.
Let no one harbor treacherous thoughts,
For Heaven observes from above.
Gathering a great army to defeat Shang,
Achieving unparalleled success.
King Cheng acknowledged his uncle,

Appointed his eldest son as Marquis,
Ruling the state of Lu as its lord.
Expanding the vast territory,
Assisting the Zhou dynasty as a shield.

Appointing Duke Bo as Lord of Lu,
Establishing a fief in the east of Zhou.
Bestowing mountains, rivers, and lands,
And small states as vassals.
The grandson of Duke Zhou, Duke Xie of Lu,
The son of Duke Zhuang, continues the ancestral glory.
The dragon banners proceed in ritual,
Six-rein chariots slowly advance.
Spring and Autumn ceremonies never cease,
Seasonal offerings punctually given.
Worshipping the luminous Heavenly Lord,
And venerating the great Houji.
Presenting red cattle as offerings,
Respectfully inviting the deities to partake.
May the spirits bestow abundant blessings,
Upon the illustrious ancestors Zhou Gongdan,
And grant blessings and protection to you.

In autumn, the Tasting Ceremony is held,
Cattle are penned and fed.
White pigs and red cattle are offered,
Their forms are used for wine containers, melodiously
ringing.
Removing the fur and roasting pig meat for stew,
Filling bamboo bowls with various legumes.
The scene is grand, with myriad dances,
Filial descendants blessed with auspiciousness.
May your state prosper and flourish,
May you enjoy longevity and well-being.
May the spirits bless your eastern realm,
May Lu's foundation forever endure.
Like the mountains, unwavering and steadfast,

Like the flowing waters, unshaken.

The Duke of Lu has a thousand chariots,
Spears wrapped with green silk, adorned with red tassels.
He is equipped with double spears and double bows.
Lu's infantry numbers thirty thousand strong,
Decked in shell armor with red cords.
Soldiers stand in formation, layer upon layer.
To deter Rong and Di, to punish Jing and Shu,
None dare to come and display their might.
May your state be eternally prosperous,
May you enjoy longevity and abundant years.
Gray hair and black back, unparalleled in longevity,
Among those of advanced age, you are preeminent.
May your state be great and vast,
May your old age be boundless.
You shall enjoy myriad years,
In good health and longevity.

Tai Mountain stands high and majestic,
Lu people revere it the most.
With Turtle Mountain and Meng Mountain,
The borders of the state extend far to the east.
As for the smaller states along the coast,
The Huai and Di tribes all submit.
None dare to resist the submission,
All obey Lu's commands.

Heaven grants the Duke of Lu great blessings,
Preserving his health and the state of Dong Lu.
Constant cities and Xucheng are within his domain,
Reclaiming the old territory of Duke Gong.
Duke of Lu, joyful, hosts a feast,
With his virtuous wife and venerable mother.
The officials and ministers are harmonious,
Each with their own territory.
Having received numerous blessings,

He rejuvenates with newly grown teeth.

On Mount Cuilai, there are tall pine trees,
On Mount Xin, there are green cypresses.
The trees are felled and sawn into beams,
Used as the structural framework.
Pine beams and square pillars, sturdy and long,
The palace is grand, spacious, and bright.
The new temple stands tall beside it.
Lord Xi composed this poem,
A monumental work, powerful and magnificent,
Hailed and admired by the people.

SHANG SONG (商颂)

The "Shang Song" is also known as the "Song Song."
After King Wu defeated the Shang dynasty, he enfeoffed
Wei Ziqi, the half-brother of King Zhou, in the state of
Song. Rituals and music were performed to honor the
ancestors of the Shang dynasty. The "Shang Song" consists
of five poems and belongs to the Spring and Autumn period.
It originated in the region around Henan Shangqiu, the
capital of the Shang dynasty during the Spring and Autumn
period.

NA (那)

How splendid and grand it is,
To raise our drums high.
The drums resound with a deep boom,
Entertaining our ancestors.
Tang's descendants pray and offer sacrifices,
Grant us smooth and successful endeavors.
The drums resound with profound echoes,
The sheng and guan play harmonious tunes.
The melodies are coordinated and peaceful,
Responding to the sounds of chimes.
Ah! Descendants of the illustrious Shang Tang,
The music of our sacrificial rites is truly enchanting.
The grand bells and drums resonate powerfully,
As people dance gracefully.
We invite distinguished guests,
And everyone is delighted with joy.
Since ancient times,
Our forefathers established these rituals.
Morning and evening, with warmth and reverence,
During the sacrifices, we are devout and cautious.
Autumn and winter sacrifices, please attend,
Tang's descendants sincerely express our feelings.

LIEZU (烈祖)

We praise our ancestors for their boundless achievements,
Leaving behind great blessings.
Multiple blessings without bounds,
Passed down to the present-day king.
Clear and fine wine for you to enjoy,
Bestowing upon us enduring blessings.
Also, the harmonious meat soup,
With balanced flavors and a delightful taste.
Silently, we offer prayers, tranquilly and silently,
The music temporarily pauses, serene and peaceful.
May the gods grant me longevity,
With gray hair and a back like a rainbow.
Gold ornaments, scales, and horse-drawn chariots,
Eight phoenix bells resound with a clear jingle.
The feudal lords come to the temple to make offerings,
Under the mandate of Zhou, they receive vast territories.
Peace, joy, and contentment descend from the heavens,
Abundant harvests fill the granaries.
The spirits descend to enjoy the offerings,
Granting us boundless happiness.
Autumn and winter sacrifices, please accept,
The descendants of Shang Tang offer their respect.

XUANNIAO (玄鸟)

By the mandate of Heaven, the Xuanniao descends to the human world,

Jiandi gives birth to the ancestors of the Shang.

The vast lands of the Yin Shang dynasty have no boundaries,

The ancient emperor bestows the mandate upon King Tang.

He conquers the four corners of the world,

Exercising authority over the feudal lords,

Possessing the Nine Provinces within his domain.

The early rulers of the Shang dynasty, both kings and ancestors,

Receive the mandate of Heaven without slackening,

Especially King Wuding, this virtuous king.

This descendant is King Wuding,

Achieving brilliance and success in all endeavors.

Ten chariots with dragon flags,

Abundant food offered in the sacrifices.

The territory spans thousands of miles,

The people live in peace in this land.

Expanding the territory to reach the four seas,

The feudal lords all come to pay homage to the King of Shang,

Submitting and gathering under the lords.

The Jing Mountain surrounds the Yellow River,

The kings of the Yin Shang dynasty receive the mandate without any obstacles,

Enjoying eternal fortune and blessings.

LONG HAIR (长发)

The great sage and wisdom belong to our Shang,
Prosperity lasting long, with eternal auspiciousness.
The vast floodwaters flowed for ages,
But Great Yu managed and established order in all directions.
Distant powerful nations became borderlands,
Expanding our territory far and wide.
There was Lady Jiang in her prime,
And by the will of the gods, she bore a son to establish the Yin Shang.

Our first ancestor, King Xuan, was truly wise,
Small states submitted to his command,
And even great states followed his orders.
Adhering to customs without deviation,
He conducted inspections throughout the land to govern wisely.
The achievements of our ancestors shine brightly,
All the vassals beyond the seas obey his command.

Our ancestors never violated the mandate of Heaven,
Passed down to King Tang, whose achievements were fulfilled.
King Tang was born at the right time,
His wisdom and prudence grew day by day.
He invited the spirits to bless and protect,
With great respect and sincerity towards the gods,
The gods appointed him as the exemplar.

Accepting the laws of Heaven, both great and small,

As a model for all the feudal lords,
Bestowed with a name by the heavens.
Without the need for competition, without haste,
Without the need to be forceful or too gentle,
His governance was generous and excellent,
With blessings and prosperity gathered like hills.

Accepting the laws of Heaven, both great and small,
The vassals of various states received protection,
Blessings from the heavens, honor bestowed upon us.
Displaying the might of the spirits and achieving victories,
Never shaken, never faltering,
Fearless and resolute,
Gathering endless blessings.

King Tang raised an army to defeat King Jie of Xia,
Wielding a mighty axe with courage like a tiger.
The military prowess blazed like a fierce fire,
No one dared to obstruct him.
A tree with three branches from one root,
He would not allow it to grow any larger.
The Nine Provinces became unified from then on,
Wei and Guo, the states, were subdued,
And Kunwu and Xia Jie were captured.

In the middle of King Tang's reign,
The nation grew strong, and the enterprise flourished.
Tang was a sincere and trustworthy emperor,
The heavens granted him wise ministers.
The wise minister was A Heng,
Assisting King Tang in achieving great deeds.

YIN WU (殷武)

King Wu of Yin was truly valiant,
He vigorously campaigned against fierce Jing and Chu.
Deep into the treacherous terrain of Chu,
The entire Chu army was captured.
The territory governed by the Chu state,
Was greatly achieved by the grandson of King Tang.

This small state of Jing and Chu,
Resides in the southern region of our country.
In the past, our distant ancestor was King Tang,
Even the powerful Di and Qiang tribes,
Dared not withhold tribute from our king,
Dared not abstain from paying respects to our king,
Throughout the world, the reverence was for the Yin Shang.

Heaven commanded all the feudal lords,
And at Yu's flood control site, he built the capital city.
Every year, they paid respects to our Shang king,
Without reprimand, avoiding calamities,
Diligently farming and not forgetting their toil.

Heaven commanded his descent to the mortal world,
And the people respected his awe-inspiring presence.
They dared not transgress customs or indulge,
They dared not be negligent or idle.
King Wu commanded the states of the world,
Each to safeguard their territory, boundless blessings.

The Shang capital is strict and flourishing,

An exemplary model for the feudal lords from all directions.
Renowned throughout the world,
Shining brightly and manifesting its divine power.
The spirits bestow longevity and peace,
Blessing future generations with eternal prosperity.

Climbing to the summit of the towering Jing Mountain,
Pine and cypress stand tall and lush.
Cutting and transporting them to the capital,
They were hewn into usable materials.
The pine beams are straight and long,
The rows of pillars are thick and robust,
The ancestral temple is constructed for the gods to enjoy.

ABOUT THE AUTHOR

The "Classic of Poetry," known as the "Shi Jing" in Chinese, is a collection of ancient Chinese poetry that lacks a single attributed author. Instead, it serves as a representation of the collective voices and emotions of the Chinese people spanning several centuries. Composed during the early Zhou Dynasty (11th-7th century BCE) and even earlier, these timeless verses stand as a testament to the artistic and cultural richness of ancient China. The poets who contributed to this anthology remain anonymous, but their words have indelibly marked Chinese literature. Through their verses, they skillfully captured the essence of their era, providing a window into the hopes, dreams, and experiences of generations past, thereby shaping the cultural heritage of China for millennia to come.

Printed in Great Britain
by Amazon